"You might be Gray's best man, and I might be Lola's maid of honor, but that does not mean we have to fall into some cliché by getting it on this week."

"Getting what on?"

"You know what I mean."

"I know that you kissed me."

"You kissed me!"

Cormac's smile said, *You know it. But you kissed me right on back, sweet cheeks.* He pressed away from the bar and took a step her way.

Harper's first instinct was to take a step back, knowing deep in her heart that, despite her demand to not be kissed again, if he came close enough for her to get even a whiff of his scent she'd be back to climbing him like a tree.

Dear Reader,

A Week with the Best Man is a book about home. About leaving home. Losing home. Coming home. And what it means to *be* home.

When the story opens, the hero and heroine have very definite ideas about what home means to them. Harper would say her home is where her work is, while Cormac believes his home is where his loyalties lie. Little do they know, those beliefs are about to unravel in a big way!

For me home isn't merely a location. It's a *feeling*—of comfort, of warmth, of ease. Feeling able to let go of a long-drawn-out breath. Feeling able to be yourself.

It's a feeling you get when in certain places and around certain people.

Curled up in a nook, with a book, anywhere in the world, I feel at home. Then again, the moment I set foot in New York City, I also feel at home. When the school bell tolls and I know I'll see my babies any minute, I'm so close to coming home I can taste it.

I loved watching Harper and Cormac figure out what home really means to them, and I hope you do, too!

Love,

Ally xxx

AllyBlake.com

A Week with the Best Man

Ally Blake

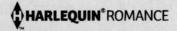

Recycling programs
for this product may
not exist in your area.

ISBN-13: 978-1-335-49944-8

A Week with the Best Man

First North American publication 2019

Copyright © 2019 by Ally Blake

www.Harlequin.com

Printed in U.S.A.

Australian author **Ally Blake** loves reading and strong coffee, porch swings and dappled sunshine, beautiful notebooks and soft, dark pencils. Her inquisitive, rambunctious, spectacular children are her exquisite delights. And she adores writing love stories so much she'd write them even if nobody else read them. No wonder, then, having sold over four million copies of her romance novels worldwide, Ally is living her bliss. Find out more about Ally's books at allyblake.com.

Books by Ally Blake

Harlequin Romance

Visit the Author Profile page
at Harlequin.com for more titles.

To the people and places that make me feel like I'm home.

CHAPTER ONE

CORMAC WHARTON SAT on the curved boot of his classic car, shoes hooked a half-metre apart on the gleaming bumper, elbows resting on knees, as he watched his dog, Novak, sprint off into the small forest to his right; a streak of sleek caramel fur in search of the stick Cormac had thrown. And had been throwing for the past forty-odd minutes while he waited for the visitor to arrive.

The sound of a car belting along Beach Road beyond the high bougainvillea-drenched walls of the Chadwick estate had him sitting up, listening for a slowing engine.

Alas, it was not to be.

So, Cormac waited. And would continue to wait. For he was best man to his best mate, Grayson Chadwick, and this was wedding-related-waiting, so it was his job to help out on such occasions. Not that he wouldn't have done so under normal circumstances. It came down to friendship. Loyalty. Respect. Balance. Duty. The pillars upon which Cormac believed a person could build a good and honest life.

Harper Addison—Maid of Honour and The

Person Cormac Had Been Waiting Forty Long Minutes For—appeared to have other ideas.

With only days to spare until her sister Lola's big day, Harper had *finally* deigned to drag herself onto a plane to join them. She hadn't condescended to actually let anyone know she was even on her way until she'd landed. Then, refusing to wait for someone to pick her up in Melbourne, she'd hired a car instead to meander down the Great Ocean Road to Blue Moon Bay at her leisure.

Lola claimed she didn't mind not knowing exactly when her sister would arrive. That she understood how busy her sister was. Cormac knew better. He knew all about keeping the family peace.

A crunch of claws heralded Novak's return as the dog bolted across the bright white gravel driveway, ears flapping, fur gleaming in the summer sun, before coming to a panting halt. Her tongue lolled around the mangled stick as she looked up at him, all liquid eyes filled with adoration and trust. It was a hell of a thing, even from a dog.

"Good girl," Cormac said, and Novak carefully placed the damp stick into his upturned palm. He gave her silky ear a rub. "Ready?"

Novak's nose quivered.

"Fetch!" he called as with a flick of the wrist he launched the stick. It whistled winningly as it

soared through the air and into the bush beyond.
And then Novak was gone, a rocket of joy bounding off into the shrubs.

When Cormac looked back to the driveway it was to see an unfamiliar car pulling through the gates.

"Here we go," he murmured as with hands flat to the warmed metal he launched himself to the ground. There he twisted at the waist and stretched his arms over his head, before running his slobber-covered hands down the sides of his jeans.

Not a hire car, he saw as it rounded past him. A long black Town Car, the kind that came with a driver and windows so dark he could not see inside. For the hour-and-a-half drive from Melbourne it was a little too much. Even for Blue Moon Bay, which was not short on folk with more money than sense.

So, what did that make Harper Addison?

Cormac tried to call up a mental image of what she'd looked like in high school.

A year or two below him, wasn't she the one who had hung around the bottom of the D-Block staircase, tin in hand, collecting coins for whatever down-on-their-luck soul had appeared in the news that week? He saw unruly brunette curls, ripped jeans, smart mouth and a frown.

Lola Addison, on the other hand, was a sweetheart; bright, happy-go-lucky, with an easy irreverence. His hazy recollection of Harper felt about as far from Lola as one could get.

The Town Car pulled to a halt at the bottom of the wide stone stairs leading up to the house. A moment later a silver-haired driver in a peaked hat and black suit alighted from the car and shuffled to the back door before opening it with a flourish.

Then, like something out of a classic Hollywood flick, a woman's shoe—the colour of champagne with a heel like an ice pick—uncurled from inside the car to stab the graveled ground.

The second shoe dropped, followed by a pair of long legs.

The woman attached to the legs came last, a hand tipped with shiny black fingernails curving over the top of the door as she disregarded the outstretched hand of the driver and pulled herself to standing, slammed the door shut and stared up at the Chadwicks' house.

Not an unruly brunette, Cormac noted as sunlight flowed over sleek, caramel-blonde waves, kicking out sparks of bronze, of gold. And no ripped jeans either, but a long, fitted, expensive-looking coat—far too much for a southern summer's day—embroidered with the same champagne colour as those killer heels.

Clearly not the bolshie rebel he thought he'd remembered. Unsurprising. For him, those later high-school years were pretty much a blur.

The driver moved in to ask her a question right

as a mobile-phone tone sounded loudly in the restive silence. She stayed the driver with a hand as she answered the call with a clear, "Yes?"

Was she for real? Cormac coughed out a laugh. Then ran a hand up the back of his head as he counted down the hours until the wedding. The hours he'd have to make nice with his counterpart in the lead-up. When he could have been working. Surfing. Staring into space. Any of which would be a better use of his time.

Friendship, he reminded himself. *Loyalty. Respect. Balance. Duty.*

The driver glanced Cormac's way, his face working as if unsure what his next move ought to be. Cormac lifted his hand in a wave and half jogged towards the car to take the passenger off the poor guy's hands.

As if she'd heard his footsteps encroaching, the woman turned.

Cormac's pace slowed as if his batteries had drained, till he came to a complete stop.

For the woman was a fifties femme fatale brought to life. A swathe of shining hair curled over her right eye. Shadows slashed under high cheekbones. Full nude lips sat slightly apart, as if preparing to blow a kiss.

Cormac found himself engulfed in an instant thwack of heat. Like a donkey kick to the gut, it literally knocked the breath right out of him.

Then she flicked her hair from her face with a

single, sultry shake of her head, said something into her phone before dropping it into a structured bag hooked over one elbow, and then both of her eyes met his.

A flash of memory hit like a rogue wave, and he knew he'd remembered her right.

He saw himself bounding down the D-Block staircase with Gray, Adele, Tara and the rest of the school gang at his heels. There she was, the unruly brunette, homemade posters covered in pictures of flood or famine tacked to the post behind her, collection tin in hand, eyes locked on his with that same unrelenting intensity.

A wet snout pressed into Cormac's hand and he flinched.

Eye contact broken, he glanced down. Novak leaned against his shin, his knee, his thigh, looking at him as if he was the greatest thing on earth.

"That's my girl," he murmured, giving Novak a scratch under the chin, before pulling himself the hell together and striding over to meet the woman he'd been waiting for.

Cormac Wharton.

Of course, *his* had to be the first familiar face Harper saw upon arriving back on home soil for the first time in a decade.

Her breath had literally stuttered at the sight of him ambling towards her. It had taken every ounce of cool she had not to choke on it.

Harper glanced back towards the Chadwicks' gargantuan house, hoping Lola might still come bounding towards her, arms out, hair flying, exuberantly happy to see her. Alas, she understood what Cormac's presence meant: the Chadwicks had enlisted him to babysit. And nobody in this part of the world said no to the Chadwicks, least of all Cormac Wharton.

Her fault, she supposed, for making her arrival a surprise. But the moment she'd fulfilled her rocky last contract, she'd wanted to get on the plane and fly away as fast as she could.

Pulling herself together, Harper turned her attention back to the man in question. Dark sunglasses covered half his face. A bottle-green Henley T clung to the broadest shoulders she'd ever seen, and his jeans fit in all the right places. His haircut hadn't changed—all preppy, chestnut spikes. The sleek toffee-coloured dog trotting at his side was new.

He looked good. Then again, Cormac Wharton had always looked good. Dark-eyed, with charm to spare and a smile that lit up a room, he'd claimed the attention of every girl in school. Including, she deeply regretted, her.

"Ma'am?"

Harper turned to find her driver still standing beside the car, awaiting instructions.

"Sorry," she said, shaking her head and offering a quick smile. "Sam, wasn't it?"

"Yes, Sam's the name. And no apologies necessary. I'm used to passengers coming off long flights. May I help take your luggage inside?"

"No. Thank you. I'm not staying. Not here. This was a quick stop in case my sister was here. Seems she's not. You were kind to drive me this far, so I'll point the way to the hotel and then you can head home."

"Not at all, ma'am. It's always lovely to find myself in here. Dare say it's one of the prettiest places on earth."

The driver's smile dropped a smidge when a shadow fell over the car. A shadow in the shape of Cormac Wharton.

The back of Harper's neck prickled as it always had when he'd walked by. She shut down the sense memory, quick smart. Enough water under that bridge to require an ark.

Seeing no use in putting off the inevitable, Harper turned, bracing herself against the impact of the man, up close and personal. He'd taken off his sunglasses, hooking them over the top button on his shirt revealing an array of frightfully appealing smile lines fanning from the edges of his deep brown eyes. Then there was the sun-drenched warmth of his skin. Sooty stubble shading his jaw. And the fact that, at five-foot-nine—plus an extra four inches in heels—she had to look up.

No longer a cute jock with a knee-melting

smile, Cormac Wharton was all man. Just like that a warm flutter of attraction puffed at the dust shrouding her ancient crush.

"Cormac Wharton," she said, "as I live and breathe," her neutral tone owing to years spent working as a professional negotiator.

"Harper Addison. Good to see you." His voice was the same, if not a little deeper. Smooth with just a hint of rough that had always brushed against her impressionable teenaged insides like the tickle of a feather.

For a second, she feared he might lean in to kiss her cheek. The thought of him entering her personal space, stubble scuffing her cheek, warm skin whispering against hers, was enough for her to clench all over.

Thankfully he pulled to a stop, rocking forward on his toes before settling a good metre away. His dog stopped, sat, leaned against him. A female, for sure.

"I'd hoped Lola would be here," Harper said.

Cormac shook his head, his dark gaze not leaving hers.

She waited for an explanation. An excuse. It seemed he was content to let her wait.

"Right, then I'll head to the hotel." She turned to Sam, the driver, who moved like lightning, hand reaching out for the handle of the car door before Cormac's voice said "Stop."

Sam stopped, eyes darting between them.

Harper's gaze cut to Cormac.

He said, "Dee-Dee and Weston are expecting you to stay here."

She shot a glance at the Georgian monstrosity that was the jewel in the immoderate Chadwick Estate. It looked back at her. Or, more specifically, down on her. Dee-Dee and Weston Chadwick might be richer than Croesus, but they couldn't pay her enough to stay under their roof. Water under the bridge didn't come close.

"I've booked a suite at the Moonlight Inn for the duration," she said, softening the refusal with a smile. "I'll be perfectly comfortable there."

"Your comfort isn't my concern."

Harper's smile slipped. "Then what, exactly, is your concern?"

"Gray's comfort. Dee-Dee's and Weston's. And your sister's. Lola's had a room ready for you here for some time now, on the assumption you'd arrive sooner. Not with only days to spare."

Harper had been in transit for over twenty-four hours. And was still a mite tender after the rare, personal unpleasantness that had tinged the last negotiation job she'd completed in London.

All she wanted was to see her sister. To hug her sister. To see for herself that Lola was as deliriously happy as she said she was. And to do so beyond the long reach of the Chadwicks and their associates.

Tangling with a passive-aggressive Cormac

Wharton hadn't been on her radar. Yet he'd just up and slapped her with the trump card; the *only* thing that would make her change her mind: sisterly guilt.

Jaw aching with the effort to hold back all the retorts she'd like to fling Cormac's way, Harper turned to her driver, her voice sweet as pie as she said, "Change of plan, Sam."

Sam squared his shoulders before flicking Cormac a dark glance. "Are you certain, ma'am? If it's still your intention to leave, all you have to do is ask."

She glanced at Cormac right as his mouth twitched. Nothing more than a flicker, really. Yet it did things to his face that no other smile in the history of smiles had the power to do; pulling, like an insistent tug, right behind her belly button.

"Thank you, Sam," she said, deliberately turning her back on the younger man. "You're a true gentleman. But if my little sister wants me to stay, then that's what I'll do."

Sam clicked his heels together before heaving her suitcase and accompanying bags to the ground. She feared hauling them up the stairs to the Chadwicks' front door might do Sam in, so before he could offer she pressed a large tip into his hand and sent him on his way, hoping she'd made the right choice as she watched the car meander slowly up the long gravel drive.

"I think you have a fan there," said Cormac, his voice having dropped a notch.

Harper tuned to Cormac and held his gaze, despite the butterflies fluttering away inside her belly. "Where *is* my sister?"

"Catering check. Wedding-dress fitting. Final song choices. None of which could be moved despite how excited she was that you were finally coming home."

Harper bristled, but managed to hold her tongue.

She was well aware of how many appointments she'd missed. That video-chatting during wedding-dress-hunts wasn't the same as her being in the room, sipping champagne, while Lola stood in front of a wall of mirrors and twirled. That with their parents long gone from their lives she was all Lola had.

Lola had assured her it was *fine*. That Gray was *such* a help. That the Chadwicks were a *total* dream. That she understood Harper's calendar was too congested for her to have committed to arriving any earlier.

After all, it was the money Harper made from her meteoric rise in the field of corporate mediation that had allowed Lola to stay on in the wealthy coastal playground of Blue Moon Bay, to finish high school with her friends, to be in a position to meet someone like Grayson Chadwick in the first place.

And yet as Cormac watched her, those deep brown eyes of his unexpectedly direct, the tiny fissure he'd opened in Harper's defences cracked wider.

If she was to get through the next five minutes, much less the next week, Cormac Wharton needed to know she wasn't the same bleeding heart she'd been at school.

She could do this. For Harper played chicken for a living. And never flinched.

"You sure know a lot about planning a wedding, Cormac," she crooned, watching for his reaction.

There! The tic of a muscle in his jaw. Though it was fast swallowed by a deep groove as he offered up a close-mouthed smile. "They don't call me the best man around here for nothing. And since the maid of honour has been AWOL it's been my honour to make sure Lola is looked after too."

Oh, he was *good*.

But she was better.

She extended a smile of her own and placed a hand on her heart as she said, "Then please accept my thanks for playing cheerleader, leaning post, party planner and girlfriend until I was able to take up the mantle in person."

Cormac's mouth kicked into a deeper smile, the kind that came with eye crinkles.

That pesky little flutter flared in her belly. She clutched every muscle she could to suffocate it before it even had a chance to take a breath.

Then something wet and cold snuffled under Harper's coat and pressed against the back of her knee. With a squeak, she spun on her heel to find Cormac's beautiful dog standing behind her. Panting softly, tail wagging slowly, it looked at her with liquid brown eyes that reminded her very much of its owner.

She was surprised to find a soft, "Oh," escape her mouth.

"Harper," Cormac's voice rumbled from far too close behind her, "meet Novak. Novak, this is Harper."

"Novak?"

"After the great and glorious Kim."

"The actress? From *Vertigo*?"

A beat, then, "One and the same."

Spending more of her life in planes and hotels than her high-rise apartment, Harper didn't see a lot of dogs these days, so wasn't sure of the protocol. What could she do but wave? "Hello, Novak. Have we been ignoring you?"

Novak's tail gave a quick wag before she sat on her haunches and— *No. Surely not.*

"Is she…smiling?" Harper asked. "It looks like she's smiling. Can dogs even smile?"

She looked over her shoulder to find herself close enough to Cormac to count his lashes. There were millions of the things…long, plentiful as they framed those deep, molten-chocolate eyes.

When she didn't look away, his eyes shifted

slowly between hers, lingering a beat before shifting back. Then he smiled. Turning her thoughts to dandelion fluff.

Then suddenly he was leaning towards her, a waft of sea salt, of summer, tickling her nose. Then he leant down to grab a couple of her bags, hefting the long handles over his shoulders as if they weighed nothing, and the moment passed.

She reminded herself—stridently—that he might look like the boy she'd thought worthy of secret teenaged affections, but those affections had gone up in smoke when she'd discovered he had it in him to stick in the knife. And twist.

Harper grabbed the handles of her last couple of bags and took a discreet step away.

Not discreet enough, apparently, as Cormac's cheek kicked into a knowing smile before he said, "Could you have brought any more baggage?"

Honey, you have no idea.

"Come on, then," he said, and with that he crunched over the white gravel and up the huge front steps of the big house.

The impressive Georgian-look manor was the first house built on the bluff over Blue Moon Bay by Weston Chadwick's father. When the next generation relocated the head office of their world-famous surf brand to the area, making the holiday estate their permanent home, the sleepy town had fast grown into a haven for wealthy families looking for a sea change.

Those who could keep up with the Chadwicks thrived. Those who couldn't…

"Come!" Cormac called.

Harper's eyebrows rose sharply, until Cormac's dog trotted up the stairs and she realised the command had not been for her.

Cormac and dog disappeared inside the double front doors as if they'd done so a thousand times before. Which they likely had.

Rumour had it that Cormac had moved into the Chadwicks' pool house right after high school. Then he and Grayson had gone on to take law together at Melbourne University before Grayson had taken his place on the board of his family's behemoth company, while Cormac opened up his own firm, servicing one client: the Chadwick family.

By the look of things, insinuating himself had been a smart move. As Harper made her way up the front steps, she wondered how much of his soul he'd had to give up to do it.

None of which made Harper feel any better about the fact that her little sister was about to marry into that world, that family, for good.

Well, she'd see about that.

Through the impressive two-storey foyer, walls unexpectedly lined with some pretty fabulous modern art, Harper kept eyes front as she followed Cormac up one side of a curling double staircase.

She found him in a large bedroom suite, leaning against a chest of drawers as he played with his dog's ear.

Her bags had been placed by a padded bench at the end of a plush king-sized bed. Sunshine poured through large windows draped with fine muslin, picking out shabby-chic furnishings and duck-egg-blue trim. A vase of fresh gardenias sent out the most glorious scent.

The room was elegant and cool. It suited her to a T.

Lola, she thought, her chest tightening, knowing Cormac hadn't been kidding. Her little sister had decorated the room with her in mind.

Harper slowly unwrapped the tie around her waist and hung her coat over the back of a padded chair, leaving her in a neat cream shift with a kick at the hem and her ubiquitous heels.

Cormac cleared his throat. She looked his way to find him watching her, his deep, rich brown eyes still holding the glint of affection he held for his hound.

"So," she managed, "am I meant to stay in here until Lola arrives, or have you been given further instruction as to what to do with me?"

Something flickered across his eyes, but was gone before she could take its measure. His hands slid into the front pockets of his jeans, framing all he had going on down there. Not that she looked. Then he pointed a thumb over his shoulder towards the door. "You hungry?"

"I'm fine," Harper lied, for she was starved. Sharing a meal was a tactic she often used mid-negotiation to soften up the combatants. And she would not be softened. Not by him.

"Then I guess we could stand here making awkward conversation till someone gets home."

Harper glanced deliberately at her watch. It was two in the afternoon. On a Monday. "I vote no."

"Hmm. Big shock." He took a step towards the door. "If we're up to our throats in my famous ham and mustard sandwiches there'll be no need to make small talk. Let me make you something. Let me feed you."

She wondered how often that line worked. By the gleam in his eye, probably every time. She actually found herself wavering towards his suggestion when a bang, a crash, a flurry of voices preceded the thunder of feet taking the stairs two at a time.

Then a whirlwind of blonde hair, yoga gear and running shoes rushed through the door and launched itself at her.

Harper's knees hit the back of her bed as she fell, laughing despite herself.

While Lola hung on tight and cried, "You're here! You're really here!"

After a quick mental scan to make sure nothing was broken, Harper hugged Lola back. Hard.

Drinking in the feel of her little sister, the hitch of her voice, the scent of her skin.

She squeezed her eyes shut tight when she felt the sting of tears. Not now. Not here. Not with an audience. Their story had always been a personal one. The two of them against the world.

"Of course I'm here," Harper said through the tight clutch at her throat. "Now get off me before I crumple. Or before you bruise yourself. You are getting married this weekend, you know."

Lola rolled away, landing on her back. "I'm getting married this weekend."

Harper hauled herself to sitting, fixed her dress and swiped both hands over her hair. "So the rumour goes."

A noise, movement, something had her looking back towards the door to find Cormac leaning in the doorway. Watching her.

When their eyes met he smiled. Just the slightest tilt of his mouth, but it filled her with butterflies all the same.

She felt her forehead tighten into a scowl.

For she'd been hanging out for this moment, this reunion with her flesh and blood, her heart and soul, her Lola, for so long.

And he—with his history, his link to the Chadwicks and his knowing eyes—was ruining everything.

"Oh, hi, Cormac!" said Lola as she crawled to

sit beside Harper on the bed, before leaning on her like a puppy. "I didn't see you there."

He tilted his chin and gave her a wink, his stance easing, his eyes softening, his entire countenance lightening.

"Have you two been getting reacquainted, then? Chatting about the good old days?"

"Not sure we had much in the way of 'old days', did we, Harper? You were—what, a year or two below me at school?"

"A year below," she said, her voice admirably even. Then, with a deliberate blink and a turn of her shoulders, she cut him out of the circle.

She took one of Lola's hands in hers and pulled it to her heart, then pressed her other hand against her little sister's face. And she drank her in like a woman starved.

The last time she'd flown Lola to holiday with her in Paris, she'd still had apple cheeks. Now they were gone. New smile lines creased the edges of her mouth. Her hair was longer too, more structured, blonder.

And shadows smudged the skin beneath her bright blue eyes.

Late nights? Not enough water? Or some deeper concern?

When their family had fallen apart all those years ago, Harper had done everything in her power to shield Lola from the worst of it. Taking every hit, fixing every problem, hiding every secret, so that Lola might simply go on, having the blessed life she'd have enjoyed otherwise.

Meaning Lola knew nothing about the part the Chadwicks had played in it all.

Here, now, seeing her sister in the flesh, Harper knew—it was time. It was time for Lola to know the truth.

"How you doing, Lolly?" Harper asked, her voice soft, her expression beseeching. "Truly."

At which point Lola's bottom lip began to quake and she burst into tears.

CHAPTER TWO

HARPER PACED UP and down the long wall of the Chadwicks' library. A clock somewhere struck seven, and her eyes flickered to the open doorway as she waited impatiently for her sister to appear.

It had been hours since Lola had burst into tears.

In the several beats it had taken Harper to come to terms with the fact her sister was sobbing in her arms, Grayson Chadwick had filled the doorway of Harper's room.

With a grunt he'd lumbered inside, climbed up onto her bed and wrapped them both in a bear hug.

At which point Lola had come up laughing, wiping her tears, looking from fiancé to sister with shining blue eyes, claiming she had no idea why she'd broken down. Likely nervous excitement, over-stimulation, and pure joy that Harper was finally here.

Harper hadn't pushed it. Not then. Not there. It had been clear Lola had not wanted to appear upset in front of Gray, which rang all kinds of fresh alarm bells.

Lola had pushed away from the bed. "You must

be exhausted. If you look in the bedside drawer you'll find I've left you a little relaxer."

"Wow, you guys are close," Gray had murmured.

Lola had smacked her fiancé, her hand bouncing off his pec. "Not that kind of relaxer, you degenerate. A *yoga nidra*. I bookmarked links to some awesome guided meditations in my favourite yoga book so she can centre herself before heading down for dinner. If I know my sister, and I do know my sister, she'll need it to handle your parents. I'll come find you in the library," she'd said, pointing a finger at Harper. "Seven p.m. sharp."

Then they'd piled out of her room, Cormac the last to go.

"A little prolonged relaxation should never be underestimated," he'd said with a nod towards her bedside drawer, before he'd caught her gaze, delivered a knockout smile, rapped a knuckled fist against the doorway and was gone.

Harper swallowed. And rolled her shoulders.

The moment she had her little sister alone Harper would get to the bottom of Lola's tears. Would see how much Lola really knew about her future in-laws. And then she would fix everything.

A scrape of shoe against floor had Harper turning to the library door and once again staring down Cormac Wharton.

He'd changed into a charcoal suit, sharp white shirt open at the neck, no tie. He looked slick and relaxed. Debonair and yet with the unshaved scruff on his jaw a little rough around the edges. Forcing her to admit—if only to herself—that, while the boy had been swoon-worthy, the man was a far more dangerous beast.

She said nothing as she waited for his gaze to finish its travels over her.

She'd chosen a fortifying dress in which to meet the Chadwicks; midnight-blue and dramatically detailed, with a full skirt and fitted bodice, the sharp horizontal neckline and long sleeves leaving neck and shoulders bare.

Cormac's eyes paused at her ankles, her waist, her décolletage, before they swept swiftly back to hers. Her breath snagged in her throat as their gazes clashed.

"Evening, Harper," he said as he prowled into the room.

She nodded, not yet trusting her voice. And began to pace as well. "No sign of Lola on your way down?"

"I wasn't upstairs. I only just arrived back."

She shot him a look. "Quick commute from the pool house?"

"The pool house? I haven't stayed there in years. How did you even know about the pool house?"

Dammit. Harper feigned interest in the wall of books when her attention was wholly on where he was in the room relative to her. "Lola talks. She keeps me up-to-date with the goings on in Blue Moon Bay."

"But that was before Lola's time. You been keeping tabs on me, Harper?"

Double dammit.

"Hardly."

Cormac stopped prowling to flick a speck of lint off the back of a chair and she came to a halt. When he began pacing once more, so did she. The smile tugging at the corners of his eyes grew into a grin as it became all too obvious they were chasing one another around the couch.

Harper sat on the soft leather lounge and reached down to pick up a book from the coffee table, as if she'd been planning to do so the entire time.

Cormac moved to take the other end of the same chair, lifting an ankle to rest it on a knee, stretching a lazy arm across the back of the seat, his fingers curled mere inches from her bare shoulder. "I wouldn't have picked you as a fan of bird-watching."

"Hmm?"

Cormac motioned to the book she was pretending to admire.

She placed it back on the table and gritted her teeth.

"You're right about Lola," Cormac said.

Harper couldn't help herself; she glanced his

way, cocking a solitary eyebrow to show her care in anything he had to say was limited.

"She talks," he said. "She talks a lot about you."

"And I talk a lot about her." Or she used to. Harper struggled to remember the last time she'd met someone new, someone she felt comfortable enough to talk about her sister with. "She's my everything. And has been for a very long time. The fact that we live on opposite sides of the world hasn't changed that."

"I'm going to tell you what she says about you too," said Cormac, "because you looked a little delicate when we left you in your room earlier. Like you could do with a boost."

Harper opened her mouth to tell him where he could put his boost, but Cormac got there first.

He leaned forward, resting his elbows on his knees, and looked back at her as he said, "I've never met anyone as proud of another person as Lola is of you."

Harper's mouth slowly closed.

"She talks so highly of your work, your ambition, how much you've sacrificed for her, we'd be forgiven for believing the sun shone out of your very eyes."

Harper shifted on the seat. Blamed the softness of the cushions.

"She loves telling the story of how you didn't freak out when she ditched her physio degree with a semester to go, even though you'd paid her way through uni. Goes on and on about how amazing you are. How happy she is that you're her sister."

He stopped there, as if waiting to see her reaction. As if he knew exactly how much she'd "freaked out" behind closed doors. And she had—calculating the costs, the overtime she'd put in to pay for it all, worrying how Lola might create a future for herself instead.

Only the relief in Lola's voice, the joy, as she'd spoken about her decision had brought Harper's outrage level down from eleven to a solid seven, which was pretty much her baseline.

Cormac's gaze remained direct and unrelenting.

If she'd managed to keep her frustration and disappointment from Lola, then she'd damn well keep it from him. Her smile was worthy of the Mona Lisa as she said, "It's true. I am amazing."

A muscle flickered in Cormac's cheek. "So it would seem."

"Yet after what happened upstairs earlier, would you say that my little sister is truly happy?"

His eyes narrowed, and slowly, slowly he leant back in the chair. Then he waved a hand in the air and asked, "What is happiness?"

When Harper realised she didn't have a ready answer, she said, "I imagine it's different things to different people."

"Then for me it's a hot morning, an empty beach and a long wave."

Harper cocked an eyebrow.

"There's a *chance*," said Cormac, "it could be the exact same ingredients for Lola, but you'd have to ask her yourself."

And she would. When she could get her sister all to herself for any length of time. Till then...

"Look, I know you're in deep with the Chadwick family, so I'm talking to the wrong person about this, but right now you're all I've got. I need to know that Lola's okay. I need to know that she's making the right decision."

Cormac breathed out long and slow. She could all but see him picking her words apart and putting them back together in his mind. Then he said, "And if I said I couldn't make any promises, what exactly would you do about it?"

Harper opened her mouth to tell Cormac exactly what she would do, when Cormac looked at something over Harper's shoulder. His face creased into a smile. With teeth. And eye crinkles. And pleasure. Before he pulled himself to standing.

"Well, if it isn't the folks of the groom!" Cormac said, holding his arms wide.

Every question fled from Harper's head as she spun so fast her neck cracked, giving her no time at all to pull herself together before Weston and Dee-Dee Chadwick glided into the room, leaving her unprepared for how overwhelming it was to see them again.

They looked much as she remembered them.

More grey in the hair, of course. More weather around the eyes. But still dripping money and success and ease. As if they had not a care in the world.

Harper was too busy noting the deep smile creases branching out from the edges of Weston Chadwick's bright blue eyes as he took Cormac in a long hug, a hug fit for a son, to see Dee-Dee coming for her.

Cool, ring-clad fingers gripped Harper's upper arms, pulling Harper to Dee-Dee's cheek. "Darling Harper. We are all so glad that you're finally here."

There was that *finally* word again. Had they made a pact to use it any chance they had?

Dee-Dee turned Harper this way and that. "Aren't you an absolute treat? Not much of Lola in you, but enough. In the eyes, perhaps. And, no doubt, the heart."

Floaty, blonde and elegant, Dee-Dee Chadwick had an unexpectedly kind touch. Warm. Enveloping. Motherly. Not that Harper would know. She hadn't seen her own mother since she was five.

The urge overcame her to twist away. To gain distance. Only her years spent as a star player in the field of corporate manoeuvring had taught Harper the value in smiling politely. While plotting quietly.

"Thank you for putting me up, Mrs Chadwick. Though I'd have been fine staying in a hotel—"

"Nonsense. We are to be family after all. And no calling me Mrs Chadwick. It's Dee-Dee."

"Then thank you, Dee-Dee," Harper managed, right as Lola traipsed through the wide doorway, mouthing *Sorry!* as she dragged Gray into the room.

Harper shook her head and mouthed *It's okay.*

"Weston, darling," said Dee-Dee. "Stop talking business, this is a family gathering. Come meet Lola's sister, Harper. Fresh in from her high-powered job in Dubai."

"High-powered, you say," said Weston as he ambled to Dee-Dee's side, placing a hand in the small of his wife's back as he looked into Harper's eyes.

Harper's breath burned in her lungs. Her back teeth ground together. Every inch of her skin felt as if it were crawling in microscopic bugs. For this man had been the cause of so much pain in her family. Did he remember? Did he care?

"She's a corporate negotiator," said Lola, sidling up beside them, her hand still locked tight in the crook of Gray's elbow.

"For?" Weston asked, attention already beginning to slide away.

Harper knew just how to get it back. "The highest bidder."

Weston blinked and seemed to see her for the first time. "That so?"

Harper wondered if Weston Chadwick recognised her father in her eyes. In her heart.

"And isn't she luminous?" Dee-Dee gushed. "Look at her skin."

"A benefit of not living under the Australian sun all your life," said Weston, his deeply tanned skin creasing as he smiled.

All Harper could think was that the only reason she'd had to leave this place was in order to chase the highest bidders, was so that she'd make enough money to provide Lola with every opportunity the Chadwicks had been able to gift their son. And the only reason that had become her responsibility was because of him. Her sister's future father-in-law.

"And that dress," said Dee-Dee, cheerfully. "So striking. Not that Harper wouldn't look just as beautiful in a hessian sack." Dee-Dee looked around for agreement just as Cormac moved into her line of sight. "Cormac, wouldn't Harper look lovely even in a hessian sack?"

Cormac glanced around the group before his gaze landed on Harper. She still couldn't get used to it; those familiar deep brown eyes looking right at her.

It was a relief when he broke eye contact to do as Dee-Dee requested and determine whether she would look good in a hessian sack. His eyes dancing over her with speed and ease. Nothing at all untoward to an untrained eye.

Only Harper read body language for a living, noting the rise and fall of his chest, the flaring of his nostrils, the way his throat worked.

Cormac liked what he saw.

Seeing that flare of attraction in the eyes of any other man, she'd have been flattered and moved on. In the eyes of Cormac Wharton it was a threat to life as she knew it.

Harper shook her head just a fraction. Please, no. Don't go there. Don't answer. Don't make this week more complicated than it already is.

Cormac smiled, his voice a rough rumble that skittered down Harper's arms as he said, "I for one would love to see Harper in a hessian sack."

Gray's laughter was like a sonic boom. Though he quickly sank into his gargantuan shoulders when his mother slanted him a Look.

"I am truly disappointed in all of you. Harper is going to think we are a bunch of yokels," said Dee-Dee, pointing a finger at each man in her midst.

"Not at all," Harper said, hoping they'd all now move on.

She had no problem being centre of attention, but only when she was prepared, armed with not a single question she did not already know the answer to. And Cormac's *And if I said I couldn't make any promises, what exactly would you do about it?* rang in her head like a promise. Or a portent.

Lola cleared her throat. "Sorry to break up the fun, but after all the wedding stuff I did today I'm famished." She winked at Harper, who could not have loved her sister more.

"Of course," said Dee-Dee. "Let's head into dinner." She took her husband's arm as he escorted her from the room.

Then Lola put her hand through Gray's elbow and allowed herself to be swept out the door as well, like something out of a royal procession.

"Miss Addison?"

Harper turned to find Cormac beside her—eyes front, one arm behind his back, the other crooked her way. As if he'd read her mind.

She laughed before she even felt it coming. Then, with a long outrush of breath, she placed her hand in the proffered elbow.

Though she took the first step, leading him out of the room.

But his legs were longer, and he wasn't wearing heels, meaning soon he was a smidge in front. So she picked up the pace. He lengthened his strides to match. And soon they found themselves all but jogging.

When Harper's high heel caught on a knot in a rug and she had to grip on to Cormac's arm to steady herself, Cormac shot her a look.

Giving in?

Never.

Yet they called a silent truce. For now. Walking at a sensible pace.

And in the silence Harper felt the warmth of him beneath her hand, even through the layers of clothing. Felt his leg as it brushed against her skirt. Felt her pulse quicken when he let go a quick hard breath, as if he too was unduly affected by their proximity.

Not that it mattered. All that mattered was Lola. Making sure she was happy. And that she would continue to be so once Harper left. Meaning she had to get to the bottom of Cormac's cryptic quip while she had the chance.

She licked her lips. Swallowed. And said, "Cormac?"

He glanced down at her, catching her up in his deep, warm brown eyes. And for the life of her she couldn't remember what she'd been about to say.

When an eyebrow cocked and a smile started tugging at his mouth, she had to say something. She went with, "How far away is the dining room?"

"It's a big house." Cormac's cheek twitched, bringing his dimple out to play. *Have mercy.*

Whatever he saw in her eyes made him breathe deep. Then his gaze travelled down her cheek, her neck, pausing on her dress. His voice dropped a fraction as he said, "You didn't actually pack a hessian sack, did you?"

Harper shot him a look that would flay the top

layer of skin off a less self-assured man. While Cormac only grinned. A quick flash of teeth that had her heart slamming against her ribs, hard enough to make her wince.

"Good," he said. "For a second there I thought I'd have to track one down too in an effort at maid-of-honour-best-man solidarity."

"No need," she said. "For the sack or the solidarity."

"Is that so?"

"You stand for Gray. I stand for Lola."

"There was I, thinking that's the same thing. Why do I get the feeling you don't?"

Right. *That* was what she wanted to talk to him about. "Earlier, before the Chadwicks arrived, when I asked if you thought Lola was happy, that she would be okay, what did you mean when you said you couldn't make any promises?"

Cormac lifted his spare hand to run it up the back of his neck. A sign of frustration, no doubt. With her. But it wasn't her job to make his life easier. It was her job to protect her sister.

"You're not going to cause trouble this week." It was a statement, not a question.

"I'm not a troublemaker, Cormac. I'm a fixer."

Cormac's gaze was unreadable.

Voices murmured ahead as they neared the dining room; a long table covered in elegant settings of fine china and huge floral centrepieces was visible through a pair of double doors.

"Who else is coming?"

"Just us."

"All that view is missing is a pair of armoured servants holding swords," Harper muttered.

"Night off."

"Ah."

Harper's pace slowed, the thought of having to play nice with the Chadwicks turning her legs to jelly. She may even have tightened her grip on Cormac's arm.

She felt Cormac's gaze slide to hers before his voice came to her, low and slow. "Harper."

"Mmm?"

"Dee-Dee was right. Even without the hessian sack, you look immoderately beautiful tonight."

Harper's gaze skittered to his. She hadn't needed to hear it to know Cormac was thinking it, for so far he'd not felt a need to hide behind propriety. Yet hearing those words from that mouth were the worst kind of bittersweet.

She'd have melted if he'd as much as gifted her a smile when she was sixteen. Now a distraction of this kind was the very last thing she needed.

When she said nothing, he went on. "And by immoderately, I mean unfairly. With relish. As if to dazzle. To create shock and awe. Why do I get the feeling this is your version of playing dirty?"

Because you're too smart for your own good.

Harper thought she might have found an ally, but she'd thought wrong. Cormac Wharton would have to be watched, and handled, very carefully indeed.

She lifted a hand to fuss with the perfectly straight lapel of Cormac's jacket. "For a small-town boy, you clean up okay yourself."

After the briefest of beats, Cormac murmured, "Look at that. We can play nice."

And he leaned in to her, just a fraction. Enough that she was forced to flatten her hand against his chest. Felt the steady thump of a strong heart through her fingers as they stood, toe to toe. Who would flinch first? Not Harper. Never Harper.

"Hurry up, you two!" Lola called from inside the dining room.

Harper pulled her hand away right as Cormac leant back. The game a draw. Though the skin of her palm tingled as if she'd held it too close to an open fire.

Something flashed across Cormac's face before he hid it behind a smile. Then, sweeping an arm ahead of him, he said, "After you, my lady."

Harper couldn't help herself; she curtsied, earning an ear-to-ear grin that had her blinking to clear her eyes, before they joined the others.

CHAPTER THREE

HARPER DID NOT sleep well.

The bed was wonderful, the sheets soft and heavy, the mattress the perfect level of firmness.

And yet her dreams sent her tossing and turning.

Dreams of Lola chained to the floor à la Princess Leia in Jabba's palace, while the Chadwicks laughed and shovelled mounds of exotic food into their gobs.

Dreams of waking and not knowing which time zone she was in. Or which city. Whose bed.

Dreams of deep, dark eyes, a smile that made her knees turn to water and a mouth carved by the gods.

She'd woken with a start, sheets tangled around her limbs, sweat sheening her skin.

After a quick shower, liberal use of her serious wasabi eye drops and a strong black coffee by way of the Chadwicks' day chef—yes, *day chef*—she put on her face, skinny grey jeans, delicate cream heels and a frilled white top. With a yawn, she tossed the necessities into her buttery leather tote and made her way downstairs to find Lola bouncing around the foyer a mite before half past eight.

Lola barrelled into Harper's arms, wrapping her in such a hug she nearly tipped them both over backwards. Harper soon realised how long it had been since she'd experienced prolonged human contact, shaking hands with a room full of suits before dismantling them across a boardroom table notwithstanding.

When Harper peeled herself away the return of lung function brought forth another yawn.

"It's the sea air," Lola said with a grin. "It's therapeutic. Calming enough, even you might relax."

Harper poked out her tongue. "I grew up here, remember."

"Oh, right. I'd forgotten you were ever a child." Lola nudged Harper with a shoulder. "Now, I get you don't feel the same way about Blue Moon Bay as I do. Fair enough, too. I was too young to remember Mum leaving, or to fully understand the repercussions when Dad made such a hash of things."

At Lola's casual mention of the defining moments of Harper's young life she took the hits. As she always had. Keeping Lola protected from the worst of it. Only now she hoped she hadn't been too thorough at keeping her in the dark.

Lola went on, oblivious, "Today is my chance to rectify that. To help you see the place through fresh eyes. To undertand how deeply I appreciate everything you've done for me in helping me follow my bliss. Why being here, being a part of this community, being a yoga teacher, being Gray's wife, beats making big bucks working nine-to-five somewhere."

Lola's eyes widened as she realised her faux pas. "Not that there's anything wrong with nine-to-five! It's just not *my* thing."

Harper laughed. She hadn't worked less than an eighty-hour week in as long as she could remember.

Which was okay, because the career Harper had forged out of necessity was her bliss.

She loved the satisfaction that came with taking what seemed like an untenable situation and finding a way to make all parties happy. Or at the very least come to an agreement. No ambiguity. Complete transparency. A deal signed. She also loved that it paid more than enough for her to give her little sister whatever life she wanted, no matter how different it was from her own.

"So fresh eyes, hey?"

Lola clapped her hands together and bounded on the balls of her feet. "Yes! It's going to be great. We'll do some wedding stuff along the way—to the tailor to check out our dresses, and a bar to check out the band who'll be rocking the wedding. But I also have a few secret plans to make you fall in love with Blue Moon Bay."

"Did you say *band*?"

"Only the best band in the bay."

"And the Chadwicks are okay with that?"

"Of course they are." There was no glancing away. No fussing with her thumbnails. No signs that she was lying and the Chadwicks were actually horror in-laws.

Yet the back of Harper's neck tingled.

The Chadwicks were as good as royalty in this community. And they had one child. One *son*. There was no dimension she could imagine in which they would not impose their influence over his wedding.

Then there was the fact they had refused to let Harper pay a cent towards the big day, asking for her blessing to allow them to pay for it all.

But what if it went deeper than that? What if they were doing so out of guilt? Was this their way of trying to rectify their part in the mess of years before? If so it wasn't nearly enough.

It took Harper's elite-level self-control to say, "I imagine a string quartet to be more to their taste. Or the Melbourne Symphony Orchestra."

Lola blinked. "Possibly. But it's my wedding."

"Yours and Gray's."

"He did his part with the proposing and being so gorgeous I had to marry him." Lola took Harper by both hands. "Harps, everything is fine. Everything is fabulous! You're so used to fighting for me you're looking for bad guys to smite. But I'm happy. This will be the wedding of my dreams."

The thing was, apart from the waterworks the

day before, Lola did seem happy. And so very young.

It was early days. Better to eke out the truth rather than smack Lola over the head with it. Harper hooked her arm through Lola's elbow and said, "So let's do this."

Lola dragged her through the double-storey foyer, and out the front door. At which point Harper took a literal step back.

The same sky-blue, open-topped sports car Cormac had been sitting on the day before was now perched on the gravel outside the front door, its engine producing a throaty purr.

The man himself lounged in the driver's seat. No sitting, or slouching, for Cormac Wharton. For the gods had gifted him an overabundance of ease which only turned Harper's tension up a gear.

Cormac shifted, looked over his shoulder.

Dark sunglasses covered his eyes, bringing his jawline into relief. And his mouth. That same gorgeous mouth that had been doing things to her in her dreams that made her blush, even now.

"Our chariot awaits!" Lola proclaimed, her good cheer carrying on the wind as she dragged Harper down the stairs. Then she leapt over the car door to sit in the back seat alongside Novak, the dog, leaving the front passenger spot for Harper.

"Morning, ladies," Cormac rumbled.

"Hey, Mac," Lola sing-songed. "Thanks for the lift."

"You bet. Harper?"

Harper was busy trying to figure out how to get in the damn car as it seemed to have no door handles. Cormac opened the door from the inside, the muscles in his tanned forearm bunching winningly.

With a smile that felt like more of a wince, Harper slid onto the soft cream seat to find the leather already warmed by the biting southern sun. A subtle breeze kicked at her hair until it stuck to her lipstick. And she could feel Cormac's gaze burning a mark into her cheek.

"You all right over there?" Cormac asked, laughter lighting his deep voice.

Harper glanced sideways to find him watching her from behind his dark shades. He tilted his chin, motioning to where she held her bag like a shield. She slid it into the footwell.

With a grin, Cormac gunned the engine and took off down the drive.

"Nice car," Harper allowed.

"Nice?" he said, his face pained, before running a hand over the leather dash. "This is an original, metallic blue, 1953 Sunbeam Alpine Mark I. You can do better than *nice*."

She could. She just didn't want to. The best she would offer was, "Reminds me of the one in that movie. With Grace Kelly and Cary Grant."

"Oh, my life!" Lola said from the back seat. "Harper you have no idea what you've just done."

Harper glanced at her sister. Then at Cormac, who had dropped his sunglasses to the end of his nose to look at her as if he'd never seen her before.

"What? What did I say?"

"He's obsessed with Hitchcock movies," said Lola. *"Obsessed."*

"Right. Novak," Harper said, pointing a thumb at the dog, who wagged her thin tail.

Lola groaned. "Poor guy actually believes this is the car used in the filming of *To Catch a Thief*."

"Really?" Harper asked, unable to withhold her interest. Had Grace Kelly actually sat in this same seat? No, from memory, she had been the one driving.

"The provenance is unprovable," said Cormac, gazing dreamily over the inside of the car. "But the research I've done leads me to believe it really could be the one."

When his eyes once more found hers, they narrowed. "Don't tell me you're a sceptic."

"I'm not much of a believer in fairy-tale endings."

Cormac lifted a hand to his heart, as if he'd been shot. "I ache for you. I truly do." At which point he pushed his sunglasses back into place and slowed at the Chadwicks' front gates.

Giving Harper the chance to deal with the fact that Cormac Wharton had just told her he *ached* for her. She had to move past this erstwhile crush of hers, and fast. The man was far too astute, and if she wasn't careful he'd soon figure it out.

"Buckle up, kids," Cormac said. "The sun is out, life beckons and the waves wait for no man!"

Waves? What waves? Harper didn't have the chance to ask, as Cormac zoomed out onto Beach Road, pressing them back into their seats.

As they curved around the mouth of the bay, heading back towards town, the car rumbled smoothly beneath them, the sun filtered through the thin trees dappling the bonnet.

The air rolling in hot waves over the windscreen and whipping past Harper's face smelled of sea salt and scorched sand. Of sunscreen and coconut oil. Of bonfires and summers that lasted for ever.

"Everything okay?" came Cormac's voice.

Harper didn't realise her eyes were closed until she snapped them open.

"You sighed," he said, his voice low. "Dreamily."

Had she? "I was…lost in memory."

"That's what today's all about," said Lola, leaning forward to poke her head between them. "Harper's been away too long to remember how amazing it is here. Today's mission is to make her fall in love with Blue Moon Bay all over again."

All over again.

If she was honest her childhood had been mostly wonderful: a kaleidoscope of lazy summers and snug winters, lit with the smiles of a permanently joyful little sister and their wildly charismatic father, who'd told her daily that he loved her more than the moon and stars.

Before he'd lost everything and bolted, making it clear that love wasn't enough to tether him. She wasn't enough.

"Shouldn't be too hard," Cormac said, his warm voice sweeping away the discomfiture of those memories. "This is the best place on earth."

Harper laughed. Sure, Blue Moon Bay was ostensibly appealing with its craggy cliffs and blustery bluffs, world-famous surf beaches, stunning homes and quaint village shops, but come on.

"You disagree."

"Oh, you weren't kidding."

Cormac shot her a glance, the edge of his mouth lifting. Even a hint of that knee-melting smile made her pulse jump.

"I prefer somewhere nearer an international airport for a start. With consistent Wi-Fi coverage. A greater variety of cuisine. Style. Culture. Need I go on?"

Cormac whistled long and low. "I do believe we've been dissed."

Lola's laughter was short and sharp. "You think?"

"So, where are these havens of style of which you speak," Cormac asked. "Give us names. Paris? Verona? Madrid?"

"For a start."

Lola perked up. "What do you reckon, Mac? Is she right? Mac's been to more countries than I even knew existed. Yet he chose to come home."

What was that, now? So far as Harper knew, Cormac had left high school, moved into the Chadwicks' pool house, skated through university and found himself in a cushy position too good to give up. It seemed she'd missed some steps.

Then again, at one time he'd given her good reason to believe the worst of him.

"Is this true, Cormac?" Harper pressed. "In-between the gnarly waves, throwing a stick for your dog and babysitting for the Chadwicks, did you truly find the time to see the world?"

A muscle ticked in Cormac's jaw—a classic sign of discomfort—before he shot her a dark look. Enjoying having him on the back foot for once, Harper wriggled down into her seat and waited.

"Yeah," he said. "I truly did."

He deftly changed down through the gears as they hit the edge of the cliffs overlooking Blue Moon Bay's rugged coastline, one side of the road dropping away to a giant curving hole that seemed torn from the edge of the continent.

Harper thought he was done, until he said, "After uni I studied in England for a bit. Worked in bars, restaurants, sold balloons in Hyde Park to earn cash to backpack every chance I could."

Lola tsk-tsked. "Seriously, Mac? Way to downplay. By 'study in England' he means he went to Oxford on a Rhodes Scholarship."

Harper's gaze whipped so fast to Cormac she nearly pulled a muscle.

"It was around the time Gray and I got together," Lola added when it became clear Cormac wouldn't. "Poor Gray, pining for his friend, started coming to the gym where I worked. One day he took my yoga class and that was that. Then Cormac broke Gray's heart by not coming straight home after Oxford. Harps, remember that Christmas I couldn't come to you in Dubai?"

Harper remembered.

"Gray and I had gone to Boston to surprise Mac. Why were you there, again?"

Cormac gripped the wheel a little tighter. "My MBA."

Harper blinked. And blinked some more. And it had nothing to do with the wind.

None of this was sitting well. Like a piece from the wrong puzzle, it didn't fit into the picture she'd built up—or down—of him in her head.

And the worst of it? With the advantages he'd had, he was wasting it all. The top-class education, the comprehensive world view; he should have been living the kind of life she'd scraped and fought and bled to achieve.

So what on earth *was* he doing in Blue Moon Bay?

Looking for answers, her gaze tripped over the

dry brush covering the cliff-face, the sandy dirt spilling onto the edges of the pockmarked road as they reached the end of the bite and slowed to a stop at an intersection.

"Well," she said, motioning to a big, battered sign pointing the way to The Oldest Working Lighthouse in South-Eastern Australia. "That's gotta add bonus points."

Cormac turned to face her, his eyes hidden behind his sunglasses. But she felt his look all the same. Flat, assessing, and not altogether cool.

"Are you sassing us, Harper?"

"I'm just saying it all comes down to taste."

"Which is your way of saying we have none."

"Pretty much."

With that Cormac laughed, the sound deep and throaty and sexy as hell. Then he lifted his sunglasses onto his head, sending his hair into a mass of shaggy chestnut spikes.

"Lola," Cormac said, eyes never leaving Harper, "your sister is most definitely sassing us."

Lola said, "And yet I am not deterred."

"Mmm…" Cormac murmured, those warm, dark eyes of his holding her in their thrall. "Neither, it seems, am I."

He took off, curling around the bend and onto the long, winding stretch of road heading into town.

His expression had been light but something in the tone had Harper's heart ricocheting off her ribcage as if she was back in the grip of teenage crushdom. And, by the smile still creasing his cheek, she had the awful feeling he sensed something of it too.

Mad at herself, and him, and life in general, Harper turned bodily towards the window.

She should be better at this. She spent every working day facing down boardrooms full of powerful people with axes to grind and fear for their futures. She stood tall against their antipathy, not a single barb or sharp glance piercing her armour, she was that sure of her position.

Facing Cormac Wharton should be no different. For she was on the side of right and he was on the side of wrong and that was that.

A small voice of dissent chirped up. And for the first time that day she remembered the contract dispute she'd most recently left behind.

She'd purposely taken on a much smaller job than normal; representing a group of investors looking to buy out a small string of Italian restaurants in London that were in financial trouble with the plan to manage them more efficiently and take them international.

The original owner, the man who had started the brand from scratch, had been amenable to negotiation. His son, not so much. Especially once Harper been brought on board to end the talks quickly.

The son of the owner had somehow tracked

down her private mobile number, leaving a string
of awful messages accusing her of being soulless.
A robot. Closed off to any real human emotion.

Yes, she saw things in black and white, sepa-
rate from any emotional attachment, but that was
her forte. Her research into both businesses had
been thorough and flawless. Her recommendations equitable.

And yet those accusations had shaken her. As if
the man tapped into some deep vein of unhappy
truth she'd hidden from herself.

Once the deal was sealed she'd left without
sticking around for the after-party. Back in Dubai,
she'd packed fast and taken a car to the airport;
the bad taste in her mouth a result the negotiation
and not the fact she was heading back to Blue
Moon Bay.

And if it wasn't for Lola, her gorgeous, smushy,
beloved little Lolly-Pop, she'd never have stepped
foot in the place again.

As wounds—both fresh and ancient—throbbed
inside her, Harper closed her eyes to the sunshine
and breathed, knowing she'd need to conserve
her energy for whatever else this place threw at
her today.

Harper knew herself to be organised. She had to
be, what with international travel, shifting time
zones, having to research every client to the nth
degree, but Lola was a revelation.

The morning passed by in a blur of visits to the florist, the baker, the candlestick maker. Seriously. A local artisan had produced custom-made candlesticks wrought into the shape of driftwood for the reception table centrepieces.

While Lola chatted to the woman who was hand-printing the seating chart, encouraging her to come to a yoga class, Harper watched Cormac through the window. He stood outside the surf-board shop across the road talking to a guy with blond dreadlocks and skinny brown limbs. Novak sat on his foot, looking adoringly at her lord and master.

"The blonde or the brunette?"

Harper jumped out of her skin when Lola suddenly popped up beside her.

"Which one were you checking out?"

Harper scoffed. "Please."

Cormac made a rolling motion with his hand and the surfer dude laughed so hard he had to bend over to catch his breath.

Harper asked, "What do you think those two could possibly have to talk about?"

"Those long boards by the front door are made by one of the Chadwicks' subsidiary companies. Knowing Cormac, he's most likely checking how Dozer—the blonde—is doing. If they're selling. If he can do anything to help."

"Why would their lawyer need to do that?" Unless something untoward was going on.

"He doesn't *need* to, he just does. Cormac knows every employee by name. Every supplier too. Makes everyone in the Chadwick family of businesses feel like more than a cog in the wheel. That they are all important."

Harper narrowed her eyes. "But what's in it for him?"

Lola laughed and gave Harper a hug. "Oh, Harps, my favourite cynic. I do love you so."

A cynic? She wasn't a cynic. She was a realist. In reality people usually did things to serve their own ends. She classed herself in that group as well. Her motivations were black and white—she did what she did for Lola. Dammit, she was fine with that.

When Cormac turned to jog across the road, slowing to wave a Kombi van through in front of him, Harper quickly turned away from the window. But not before catching a knowing glint in her sister's eye.

"Ready?" Cormac asked as he strode in the door, dark eyes taking in Lola, who was trying to hide a grin, and Harper, who was trying to hide the heat that had risen in her cheeks.

"Ready as she'll ever be," said Lola, moving to hook a hand into the crook of Harper's elbow and drag her from the shop.

CHAPTER FOUR

CORMAC STOOD BY Gray's Jeep, wetsuit unzipped and hanging low from his hips as he waxed down his surfboard, not watching Harper and Lola doing yoga on the beach.

Or, to be more exact, Lola did yoga while Harper tried not to fall over. Or bend too far. Or snap in two.

"So what do you think of the elder Miss Addison?" asked Gray as he ambled around the car, wetsuit zipped up, board under one arm, half-eaten apple in the other hand.

"She's all right, I guess."

The moment the words left his mouth Cormac knew he'd played it too cool. Gray might not be as over-educated as Cormac, but he was no dummy.

Gray leaned against the car. "*All right*, you say? Sure, if a face that would once have been carved into the bow of a ship could be considered '*all right*'."

Cormac continued rubbing wax over the plane of his board.

Gray grinned. "Seems really smart too, don't you reckon? Scary smart. Quick tempered, though. A little sharp on the palate but elegant with it. Graceful but tough. Killer combination."

"Maybe you're marrying the wrong sister."

Gray laughed, delighted to have finally nudged out a response. "Nah. I'm good. I love my little bundle of sweetness and light. Harper is far too cool for the likes of me. By that I don't mean *cool*. I mean hot fury banked behind an icy mask. That one's pure kryptonite for poor saps who seek out a challenge."

Gray shivered dramatically, like a St Bernard shaking water from his coat.

While Cormac felt his gaze drag back to the women on the beach in time to see Lola performing a headstand, feet wriggling gleefully.

Harper, on the other hand, stood with her arms crossed, shaking her head, her entire body a study in tightly coiled suspicion. It ought to have been enough for him to dismiss her out of hand.

For he was easy going. Look at him, waxing a surfboard on a week day. Sure he'd done three hours of work before the rest of the gang were even awake, and he'd do more tonight once his babysitting duties were done. But he was extremely content with the balance he'd achieved in his life.

In fact, he'd have gone so far as to say he had life pretty much figured out.

Relax. Look up. Breathe. Be kind. Do good. Figure out what you love to do and do it more.

So why did seeing Harper walk out of the Chadwicks' house that morning make him feel like a racehorse locked in a stall?

Why, every time she came near, did he feel a need to brace himself, as if readying for a jolt of static shock?

Why did watching her now feel as if he was staring at sunlight glinting off the bonnet of his car, forcing him to blink against the intense bursts of light? Yet he couldn't look away.

In the distance, she squared her shoulders and lifted her chin to stare out at the horizon.

And it hit him.

The first time he'd seen *Rear Window*, he'd been fourteen years old. He still remembered the moment Grace Kelly first appeared on screen, her shadow falling ominously over Jimmy Stewart as he slept on, unsuspecting.

He'd found himself stunned by those sultry eyes, the mouth slightly open, décolletage bare as she leant in for a kiss.

But it was her cool detachment as poor Jimmy tried to lift himself out of his wheelchair to follow her kiss when she pulled away that had made him feel as though some switch had been flipped inside of him. As if he'd been given a glimpse into the mysterious, dangerous, world of Woman.

That was Harper Addison.

She was nothing so simple as a challenge. She was a tectonic shift.

"Earth to Mac," Gray said, his laughing voice now sounding as if it was coming from a mile away.

Cormac blinked and sniffed in a breath. Then he held up a hand to his face as if he'd been looking beyond the sand to the waves. "Better get cracking if we hope to find a decent curl."

"Funny, I've never seen you so intensely interested in a curl before." Then he reached out and slapped Cormac on the arm. "Relax. I get it. And I'm okay with it."

Cormac rubbed the board so hard the wax went flying out of his hand and rolled down the scrubby bank, collecting sand and dirt as it went. "Mate, I'm not hot for your fiancée's sister. Nothing is going to happen there. So get over it."

Curled darkly beneath the sudden sharp twang to his voice, Cormac heard his father. It took the edge off his aggravation as thoroughly as a bucket of iced water.

Plucking his board from the sand and hefting it under an arm gave Cormac an extra few seconds to summon up a smile. "You're projecting."

"You think?"

"Tell me you're not imagining us buying houses in the same street. Having Sunday barbeques. Our kids growing up as cousins."

Gray's eyes widened. "Whoa. I hadn't even thought that far. But how amazing would that be? You should totally marry her."

Cormac brought a hand to his chin and pretended to consider it. "Nah. I'll pass."

"Whatever you say." Gray tossed his apple core into the bush beside the car, then turned and jogged down the rickety stairs criss-crossing the dunes leading down to the beach.

Cormac breathed out hard. Closed his eyes against the sunlight a moment while he pulled himself together. Then whistled for Novak to stop investigating the scrub and follow him down the steps.

And not for the first time he thought, *Thank goodness for Gray.* A guy who'd never raised a fist to Cormac. Or even his voice. A guy whose family had been nothing but open, and warm, and welcoming, even when Cormac had been angry, confused and scared. Without them, who knew what path he'd be on now?

Which was why coming back to Blue Moon Bay had never been in question. Not really. The moment they'd offered him the job, he'd accepted. For he owed the Chadwicks more than loyalty. He owed them his life.

When Gray reached the girls he shoved his board into the sand before creeping up behind Lola and lifting her bodily, swinging her in the air.

Novak danced around them as Lola's squeal was caught on the wind.

Harper stopped mid-lunge, her hands coming up onto her hips before she shuffled her bare feet together. Her pale jeans had been rolled up to her knees. Her fussy top was now tied around her waist, leaving her in a lacy tank-top. As she heaved in a breath Cormac was gifted with a peekaboo sliver of skin and a flash of belly button.

Who knew an outie could be enough to make a man have to breathe deep in order not to embarrass himself?

Harper turned right as Cormac shifted his surfboard in front of him all the same, her long ponytail whipping around her face. Small curls had sprung up around her hairline. Her cheeks were stained with colour, her hazel eyes bright.

One of the thin straps of her top slipped down her shoulder, revealing just a hint of a curve of a strapless bra. Half-cup. Heaven help him.

"Your thing," he grunted, glancing determinedly at her shoulder.

"My what?" she asked, brow furrowing.

"Your—thing."

Words having deserted him, Cormac moved in, lifted a hand to slide her strap back into place, his knuckles grazing hot, sweat-dampened skin, before he drew his hand away.

Keeping his gaze up wasn't enough to stop his heart from pounding. To ease the blood rush behind his ears. To dampen the urge to slide the strap back off her shoulder, to run his palm over that soft, sun-kissed skin.

Harper's chest rose and fell in short sharp

breaths. Heat shimmered in her bright eyes. Mutual attraction spread like a fog, curling around them till they were both enveloped.

Then she cleared her throat, readjusted her top and shook her hair out of her eyes before going back to glaring at him for all she was worth.

What had he promised Gray? *Nothing was going to happen there.* He'd actually believed it as he'd said it. As if saying it would make it so. But, up close and personal, he knew it wouldn't be a given. It would have to be a choice.

Somehow Cormac found a last remaining scrap of cool, enough for him to dredge up a smile as he asked, "Having fun?"

Lines dug deep into the skin above her nose. "What do you reckon?"

"You know, that's the first time that you sounded like a real Aussie."

She narrowed her eyes like a cartoon villain. "What's that supposed to mean?"

Figuring baiting her had to be safer than touching her, he said, "You're all uppity-woo now. Posh-tosh with that non-accent of yours. Almost as if you've purposely scrubbed away any evidence of where you came from."

Harper's eyes went from comically narrow to wide with shock. "I'd never have imagined the day I heard Cormac Wharton say 'posh-tosh' or 'uppity-woo'. It was worth coming back just for that."

And then she laughed. The sound unexpectedly

raw, husky and brash. It shot heat straight from his ears to his groin. When her laughter subsided, it left a smile behind. The kind that kicked at just one corner of her mouth. A mouth that was pink, soft and far too kissable.

Cormac took a subtle step back, turned his surfboard horizontal, used it as a shield. "Going to have a dip?"

She glanced out at the churning waves, the wind having picked up over the past couple of hours. "You're actually going out there. Looks... dangerous."

"It is. And yet I go anyway."

She rolled her eyes. "So brave."

"Nah. Just hooked. I head out every day if I can. Ups the dopamine. Great workout. Great excuse for a big breakfast after." He patted his flat belly. Watched as her gaze went there. And stayed.

Her eyes darkened. Her jaw twitched. Her chest rose and fell again. This staying-away-from-her thing was not going to be easy. But whoever said self-sacrifice ought to be?

"This'll be my second time today, in fact. Gray slept in. So here we are."

"Gray does love his sleep," said Lola, appearing with Gray's hand in hers, before tipping up onto her toes to give her fiancé a kiss.

Cormac saw all this out of the corner of his eye, unable to keep his gaze off Harper. Meaning he didn't miss the contempt that tugged at the corner of her mouth.

It wasn't for Lola. It was clear she adored her little sister as much as Lola adored her. Meaning the disdain was all for Gray.

Cormac's sense memory snapped into gear, his muscles tightening with the readiness to step physically between a loved one and a threat. A theory he'd been skirting around until that moment shifted into sharp focus, and the final reason Harper had him feeling on edge fell into place.

Her questions about Lola the night before, asking how happy she was, had not been casual. Harper was not on board with Lola marrying Gray, and he had no doubt that over the next few days she'd do something about it.

For he'd known people of her ilk before, prepared to voice their opinion even if it made them unpopular, because being right was more important to them than being judicious.

Harper had it in her power to unhinge everything. To make Lola doubt. To cause trouble for the Chadwicks. To hurt Gray. Add enough pressure and any family could be made to tear apart.

He stepped in, ready to take action, when Lola perked up and said, "Come on, Harps, let's go for a walk. Go surf, boys. The day is still young and there is much left to do."

Harper's wince was infinitesimal. Though when her face cleared there was none of the animosity he'd seen towards his friend. Just her usual heady mix of fire and ice.

"Can we take Novak?" Lola asked.

Cormac tipped his chin up the beach and Novak took off, bolting along the sand before turning back with a "hurry up" bark. And the women followed, Harper's hips swaying hypnotically as she navigated the soft sand, caramel ponytail swinging beguilingly behind her.

"Kryptonite," Gray said, his fist exploding while he made the accompanying sound of a bomb, before running down into the water and out into the waves.

Realising he wasn't fooling anyone, Cormac watched the women work their way up the beach for a few more moments before he tore his gaze away and made his way to the water's edge.

Once knee deep he threw his board down and his body after it. It might not be the cold shower he needed, but it would have to do.

The car was relatively quiet as they rounded Beach Road on the way back to the Chadwick estate. Lola had gone in Gray's Jeep, leaving Harper and Cormac alone.

Unfortunately, it only made her more aware of Cormac in the seat beside her. The warmth of his thigh near hers. The nearness of his hand as he changed gears. The fact that she *knew* he was feeling it too.

Never in her life had she met a more confounding man.

First there was his geography. Well-travelled, and internationally educated, he chose to live in the back end of the most remote habitable continent on earth.

And she was extremely wary of how close he was to the Chadwicks.

Then there was the hurtful memory of the last thing he'd said to her all those years ago.

For some reason she got the feeling he didn't seem to like *her* very much either, yet she'd found him devouring her with a glance more than once.

Not that she'd acted any better. Watching Cormac come out of the surf, water droplets raining over him like diamonds, his chest bare, board shorts clinging to strong brown legs, she had felt as if she'd swallowed sand.

No matter the unexpected spark between them, there was nothing to be gained by revisiting her old crush. She had to be vigilant. Keep her focus tight. On Lola and the family her sister was hoping to marry into.

They hit the coastline, land dropping away to the squalling Southern Ocean on their right and rambling up into the sky to Harper's left. Shadow and light flickered over her face, forcing her to shut her eyes. And jet lag mixed with the emotional see-saw of the past couple of days finally took over.

In a sleepy half-awake state, Harper found herself once more swimming in memories. Like Polaroid pictures, the images were a little fuzzy and out of focus. But the location was clear: high school, tenth grade.

Part of the school extension programme, Harper had been able to join the year above for one class per term. Once it had been biology with Cormac.

Harper, thankfully, had been partnered with the top student in the class, an industrious girl from Torquay who bussed in every day.

Thankfully, because without her steering Harper might well have spent every lesson staring at the back of Cormac's gorgeous head.

He'd been partnered with Terence "The Bug" McIntosh. Named for the thickness of his oversized glasses.

Harper—who knew Terence a little from when she was collecting money to save the bees—knew that Terence liked the nickname. Bugs were his favourite people. But that didn't make him less ripe for the attentions of those with an eye for bullying.

While Cormac's friends made it clear they thought it hilarious he had to sit with The Bug, Cormac had ignored them all.

In fact, he'd taken the time to make friends with his lab partner—this kid half his size, with a face full of spots and interests a million miles from Cormac's own. Laughing during class, stopping to chat to him in the halls, throwing his arm around the kid's shoulders, marking him as a protected species. Together they'd delivered a hilarious and well-researched final presentation that Harper had watched with both hands over her cheeks lest the whole class see her adoration for Cormac written all over her face.

Harper came to with a start. It took a moment to remember she was in Blue Moon Bay, Cormac's car rocking beneath her as he drove her back to the Chadwick estate.

"It's the sea air," Cormac murmured.

She turned her head to find him watching the road. One arm resting on the open window, the other hand a light touch on the steering wheel.

He shot her a quick smile, and she had one last flashback to high school; a time of constant study, keeping down a weekend job, volunteering, navigating her dad's mercurial moods. Even on her most challenging days, that smile had never failed to chase her blues away.

"The sea," he repeated. "The sunshine. The fresh air. It does something to a person. On a cellular level."

She waited for a punchline. But he was serious. He wanted her to know this place was important to him.

Before she could ascertain why it mattered that she understood, they slowed, pulling around the white brick walls leading to the gravel drive of the Chadwick estate.

The Jeep had beaten them there. Lola and Gray watched Cormac and Harper pull up, all bright, guileless gazes and big, toothy smiles. The monstrous house loomed behind them.

"The two of you look like an ad for healthy, wealthy living," Harper muttered while she unclipped her old seatbelt and fiddled unsuccessfully with the door handle.

"Thanks," said Lola.

Gray burst out laughing. "Honey, I'm not entirely sure she meant that as a compliment."

Harper stopped wrestling with the handle as she caught Gray's eye. Well, well, well. Not as simple as he seems.

As if he knew exactly what she was thinking, Gray tipped his head in acknowledgement.

Before she could react, Cormac reached across her lap, grabbed the inner door handle and clicked it open.

At the wash of warmth from his nearness, his drinkable scent catching her out, Harper stilled right as he drew his hand back. The backs of his knuckles caught on the frills of her shirt before brushing lightly, softly, achingly over her breasts.

The whole thing happened in less than a second, yet Harper remained frozen. Her breath stuck in her lungs, the frills of her shirt swaying under her nose like some teasing reminder.

Then her eyes went to his.

He gave her an easy smile, no teeth, as if simply waiting for her to hop out of the car. Only the flare of awareness burning in the depths of his eyes, and the way his hand gripped and ungripped the steering wheel, indicated he'd felt the touch too.

"Thanks?" she said.

"You're welcome?" he said, copying her faulty inflection. Despite the attempt at humour, his voice was deep and throaty and coarse. The voice of a man barely holding himself together.

"Come on, Harps," Lola said, her sing-song voice coming from a million miles away.

Spell broken, Harper swallowed and hopped out of the car on shaky legs.

"We need to get changed, put on some lippy and get ready to lose several decibels of hearing."

"We're going out *again*?"

"We're going to hear the wedding band play!" Lola threw her hands in the air. Behind her Gray copied the move.

Harper heard Cormac's door shut but deliberately did not look back. Maybe that was the key. Not looking at him at all. No getting lost in those deep brown eyes. No imagining how his springy hair would feel between her fingers. No holding out for even a glimpse of that smile.

Out of sight, out of mind had worked for the past decade; it'd have to work now.

"Go make yourselves pretty, boys," Lola said. "Give us half an hour and we're all yours." Lola turned to Harper with a grin. "It'll be a double date!"

"Yay!" Harper said, throwing her hands in the air in imitation of the lovebirds, before following Lola into enemy territory to prepare for the next level of hell.

CHAPTER FIVE

HARPER SHOWERED, CHANGED into a cream bustier, black pencil skirt and pearlescent stiletto sandals, taking time to turn the beachy frizz into smooth, Veronica Lake waves. Cormac had been right in suggesting she dressed to dazzle. But she it wasn't her version of playing dirty. It was her version of armour-plating.

Gray drove this time, escorting them in his old Jeep, to the next town over—bigger, more touristy, full of bars.

Their bar—The Tide—boasted dive-bar chic, all crumbling brick and flaking black paint on the window frames. The deep base sound of rock music thumped through the walls.

Lola took Gray by the hand and dragged him past a long line of people to the front door, where a bouncer the size of a yeti stood holding a folder.

"Seth!" said Lola. "I haven't seen you in class for too long."

The bouncer took one look at her and melted. "I know, Miss Lola. I've been busy."

"How's your neck?"

"Not good."

"Come. Next week. Promise me."

He blushed. "Promise."

"Excellent. I have these three cutie-pies with me. All right?"

The bouncer's lovey-dovey smile hardened as he ran beady eyes over Gray, then Cormac. He seemed to save his longest glare for Harper.

"That's my big sister, Harper," Lola said. "She's here for my wedding this weekend. Hey, Seth, you should totally come!"

Harper opened her mouth to reprimand Lola for making such an unconsidered request. There were seating plans to consider. And catering. Fire hazards. Lola had been that way her whole child-hood—saw a tree, had to climb the tree, saw a dog, wanted the dog, even if it was at the end of someone else's lead. Their father's light ran through her blood, but thankfully none of the dark.

But then she looked to Gray. Let him be the bad guy here. For Lola was his responsibility now, or she would be come Saturday afternoon.

Gray shrugged. "Sure. The more the merrier. We'd love to have you there."

Harper gawped. Then saw the delight in Lola's eyes. Not a new kind of delight, but a warm and familiar glance. As if she knew exactly the kind of man she had and was grateful for it.

Harper felt herself soften towards the big guy. If he knew Lola that well, enough to realise how happy a yes at such a ridiculous request would make her, then maybe…

Then Harper remembered Grayson was a Chadwick. Which made him the wrong man for Lola, no matter what.

The face of the man who'd sent her the awful phone messages slid unbidden into her head, his voice cracking as he accused her of seeing in black and white. She shook him off. She did believe in absolutes. In right and wrong. In the fact that it was easy for a man to say yes when they owned the whole damn town.

"Ease down, soldier," Cormac murmured, his deep voice rolling over her, his hand clamping gently over her wrist.

She pulled her hand away, the skin burning from his touch. Shocked that her intentions had been so clear.

"Bite me," she shot back.

"Any time, anywhere."

Her gaze clashed with his. She could all but see the sparks that now seemed to be multiplying between them. She definitely felt them.

Cormac's smile was slow and smouldering. Knowing. Before he casually motioned to Seth the bouncer, who had lifted the velvet rope to let them through.

Once inside, Lola grabbed Gray by the hand again as they made their way down a long, dark hall, leaving Harper and Cormac to bring up the rear. Harper kept her distance, not wanting to make accidental physical contact again. Especially not in the dark with his *Any time, anywhere* rolling through her mind on a loop.

Until they spilled out into the bar proper. Despite its less than enticing exterior, the inside was beautifully kitted out. A large room with wood columns throughout, an empty stage at one end, a long, clean-looking bar with mirrors behind and elegant drop lighting all round.

The bouncer wasn't for naught, as the place was packed. On a Tuesday night too. That was beach living for you.

"This cosmopolitan enough for you?" Cormac asked, leaning close so he could be heard over the music.

Harper caught his scent—freshly cleaned male skin, with a tang of sea air still clinging to his hair—before she leaned determinedly away.

"It's no Cavalli Club," she said, referring to her favourite place to grab a cocktail to celebrate a contract fulfilled.

"I'd suspect nothing ever is." His smile was quick. A flash of white teeth in the darkness before he turned away, looking for Lola and Gray through the crowd. Spotting them, he reached back with a hand.

Harper stared at it.

"I won't bite," he said, not needing to lean in for Harper to understand. "Not right now anyway."

His hand closed around hers—warm and a little rough. As if perhaps he didn't spend his days merely chauffeuring bridal parties around town. And every time his skin shifted against hers she felt it. All over. As little triggers all over her skin. And waves of warmth beneath.

Chatting and charming as he went, Cormac forged a path through the crowd till he found Lola and Gray at a small reserved cocktail table near the stage.

Lola had already scored a bottle of bubbly; Gray was pouring out the glasses. When he lifted his glass and drank deeply, he caught Harper's eyes. Said, "Soda water."

Once again Harper felt the world shift a little off its axis as Gray surprised her. Had it been that obvious she'd been ready to add another sin to the list? First a Chadwick and now a drunk driver?

Harper lifted her glass to Gray's and said, "Chin-chin."

Gray grinned, lifted his glass, tapped it heartily to hers, and drank.

After one glass of the very good bubbles, Harper agreed to another. She must have been thirsty after the heat of the day, as it was gone before she remembered drinking it.

Then a tray of milky-green shots appeared from nowhere. Amarula and some peppermint liqueur; she didn't catch the name. She tried one—it was good. It would be rude not to have another.

"Isn't this fun?" Lola asked.

Harper nodded. Being out with her sister as adults wasn't something they'd managed before Harper had moved overseas. She'd been too busy studying, working to save for Lola's university, for rent, food, Lola's ski trips, surfboards, fun money and all the extras it took to fit in in Blue Moon Bay.

"What's your favourite cocktail?" Lola asked. Then, before Harper could answer, she shouted, "Pina coladas all round!" The tables near by shouted happily along with her, so Gray—with his deep pockets—ended up buying pina coladas for the entire bar.

By the time the band started up, Harper was well and truly sozzled. Her vision was hazy, her insides buzzed; she couldn't seem to stop smiling.

So glad was she to be with her sister in the flesh. So glad the bar wasn't a dive. So glad she'd picked the shoes that as comfortable as they were dazzling.

She actually felt…*happy*.

Why had she been in such a grump? Blue Moon Bay really was pretty. She'd had a lovely day re-discovering the place. Gray seemed nice, if not a little dull for her tastes. And it was becoming clear that he knew, and adored, her sister. The Chad-wicks—despite their past misdemeanours—were excellent hosts. There was nothing wrong with having your own chef! And, disruptive dreams aside, the bed was like a cloud to sleep on.

As for Cormac Wharton? Harper blinked and across the table he came into focus.

He looked *good*. More than good. Slick grey jacket over white T-shirt. Jeans that fitted just right. Thick chestnut hair in those adorable spikes. Low light creating sexy shadows under his puppy-dog brown eyes. He looked all broody and delicious, like a modern-day James Dean.

What kind of name was Cormac, though? Although she could talk...

Most of the boys at Blue Moon High had names like that. Blane. Preston. Braxton. Like the bad guys in a John Hughes movie.

Corm. Mac.

He looked up, questioning. Had she said that out loud? She sucked on her straw and squinted a smile his way.

He blinked, the broody furrows in his brows clearing as his face split into a smile. And not just any smile. *The* smile. Like sunshine on a rainy day. The moon coming out from behind a cloud. A unicorn appearing in a dell.

The one that made her heart feel as if it was locked in a fist.

Whoa. So there was happy and then there was precarious. Harper let her drink drop and breathed out long and slow.

Cormac's furrow slowly returned. He cocked

his head, questioning. But what could she say? That she'd happily look at him all night long? That she'd once thought him the most beautiful boy in the whole world? That she wondered what a girl had to do to make that *any time, anywhere* promise come true?

"Let's dance!" Lola cried, then grabbed Harper by the hand.

Needing a little cooling off, Harper took one last sip of her cocktail before reaching back with her drink. Cormac reached back and grabbed it. She gave him a grin of thanks. When he smiled back, her stomach flipped a full three-sixty degrees.

She lifted her hand to her mouth and blew him a kiss.

He blinked, reached out and caught it, and pulled it to his heart.

It was all so ridiculous Harper laughed, feeling it from her belly button to the outer reaches of her skin. Inside that happy little bliss bubble, she let Lola drag her wherever she pleased.

Which turned out to be the dance floor.

"There's a band!" Harper said, only just noticing the stage was now full.

"My wedding band!" Lola shouted, giving them a big wave.

The lead singer waved back, and the band played…something. A few somethings. All of them fabulous.

It had been so long since Harper had danced. Or listened to music on purpose. Or carved out time to just let go.

With the disco lights dancing over her eyes, the thump of the bass resounding through her bones, her sister at her side, she danced till her top stuck to her back, till the balls of her feet ached, till her body no longer felt less like a tightly wound rubber band and more like a warm, wet noodle.

What other sisterly experiences had they missed over the years? Birthdays. Work days. Drunk days. Sad days. So many hazy, lazy summers and winters so brisk it felt as if Antarctica was on your doorstep.

Harper caught Lola's eye. Then her hands. Then pulled her into a hug.

Lola stopped dancing and hugged her back.

"I love this song," Harper said.

"Love you too, Harps."

Before Harper could digest all the feelings she was feeling, Gray appeared, taking Lola's hand and sweeping her out of Harper's arms and into his own.

Watching them together Harper smiled when she felt as if she might burst into tears.

She shifted from foot to foot beside them until the buzz began to fade. Then she slunk through the crowd. Feeling squidgy. Off kilter. As if she'd left something behind.

She found Cormac at the bar, the pool of light

from the pendant lamp above carving shadows onto the strong planes of his face. When she dragged herself up onto the bar stool next to him he didn't budge. Moreover, he didn't notice.

"Hey," she said, bumping him with a shoulder. Though her sense of balance was such she didn't so much bump as lean.

Meaning when he looked over at her, she was snuggled up against him. Close enough to see every tangled eyelash. The smudges beneath his beautiful eyes. The slight bump in the bridge of his nose. The stubble fighting its way to the surface despite the fact he'd shaved. The sensual seam between his lips.

When she felt drool pooling beneath her tongue she used the bar for leverage, pushing herself away.

"Well, that was fun," she shouted. Then realised she no longer needed to as the acoustics at the bar were awesome. "The dancing. Fun. The band's really good."

"So why aren't you still out there?"

"Gray and Lola…" Harper waved a hand towards the dance floor. And felt that same sad feeling break over her again. But she didn't want to feel sad, not when she'd been feeling so good.

So she pressed her shoulders back, lifted her chin and said, "Don't you love this song?"

Cormac coughed out a laugh. For once there was no humour in it.

"Not a favourite?" Harper asked.

"Not." He took a mighty swig from his designer beer, before staring across the bar into nothing.

Harper looked around. Where was charming Cormac Wharton and what had this curmudgeonly stranger done with him?

Funnily enough, while his vibes were very much "stay away from the bear", Harper found it a relief. With no need to brace herself against the constant charm offensive, she could finally relax.

She settled more comfortably on the bar stool, caught the bartender's eye and asked for a big glass of iced water.

"Sure about that?" the bartender asked, leaning a forearm on the bar and giving her the twinkle eye. "Can't tempt you with something a little more exciting?"

He was handsome, and she was well-pickled, so she gave him the twinkle eye back. "Get me that glass of water and you'll see how excited I can be."

As the bartender poured her drink, Harper could have sworn his pecs danced, one after the other, behind his tight black T-shirt.

Then again, she couldn't exactly trust her eyesight. She felt squiffy. And hot. Her hair stuck to the back of her neck. She pulled the top of her bustier away from her chest and blew a stream of air into the gap.

When she looked back to the bartender his eyes had dropped to her chest. Oops.

Gently tugging the top of her bustier back into place, she spared a quick glance at Cormac. And got nothing. No gulp. No gawp. He was too busy staring moodily into the middle distance to score a flash.

When the glass of iced water appeared in front of her she crooked a finger at the bartender. "My friend here doesn't like this song, but I do. You can be the tiebreaker. So what's the verdict? Good song, or the worst?"

"Good song," the bartender agreed, twinkling with all he had.

"See?" Harper said, slapping Cormac on the arm.

Cormac refused to respond.

So Harper poked him in the arm. Then the shoulder.

When she went for his cheek he caught her finger in a closed fist and slowly brought it back down onto the bar.

Their eyes caught. When Harper found herself drowning in pools of melted dark chocolate she breathed in so fast, so deep, the wires inside her bustier strained against her ribs.

Out of the corner of her eye Harper noted the bartender moving away to flirt with someone else.

"You have good reflexes," she said, her voice sounding a little more awed than she'd meant.

"You're drunk," he said, one eyebrow raised, a half-smile on his face.

With her mental barrier no longer in place, Harper felt the power of it like a sucker punch, sapping the air right from her lungs.

"Pfft," she said though her lips were a little numb, so it sounded more like a raspberry. "I'm a grown woman who has had a couple of—" *several* "—legal alcoholic beverages. For which I will not apologise."

She lifted her spare hand to brush away a lock of hair that had fallen into her eyes. When it fell back into place she shook her head. When her brain jiggled like jelly she stopped.

Cormac let go of her finger and held up his hand in surrender, before lowering it to wrap around his drink.

Harper sat on her hand in an attempt to suffocate the fizzing feeling left over from his touch. "So… Cormac."

"Yes, Harper."

"Hmm? No, I mean, *Cormac*—is it a family name?"

He swallowed a sip of beer and shook his head. "My mother chose it. After Cormac McCarthy. The author."

"Me too! I mean, I wasn't named after Cormac McCarthy. Obviously. But people often believe I must have been named after Harper Lee. Though I wasn't. Which isn't the same thing at all, is it? Quite the opposite."

Harper knew she was rambling. But, now that

she'd let down her guard, she was struggling to remember where she'd put it.

"My sister got the short end of the stick there," she managed. "Being named after someone famous."

"The Kinks song?"

"Bugs Bunny's girlfriend."

Cormac shot her a look that put the bartender's twinkle eye to shame. The life force behind those deep brown eyes of his so strong, so vibrant, so rich, Harper curled her toes into her shoes to distract herself from the heat washing though her.

"So, McCarthy," she managed through a tight throat. "He wrote *The Road*, right?"

"That he did. But my mother was obsessed with one of his earlier books—*Blood Meridian*."

"Ah."

"You've read it?"

Harper read company accounts, stockholder documents, investigative reports. If she had a spare half-hour on a plane she answered correspondence, checked in with erstwhile clients. She hadn't read for pleasure in years. Which, in that moment, felt kind of sad. And again she felt a wave of a kind of lost feeling come over her—as if she was missing out.

"Have not," she admitted.

"It's a brilliant book. A modern classic. But it's not pretty. About a kid with a ken for violence, whose mother dies during childbirth."

"Jeez," Harper said on a long, loud breath before she could hold it back. "Sorry. That's..."

"Dark?"

"I was going to say intense." And unexpected.

Seeing him in high school, anyone would be forgiven for imagining his was a life full of ease, and comfort and love. After the...incident, it had made it easy to despise him, believe he had no clue what it meant to struggle.

Now she felt as if she'd peeked through a crack in his front door. That she'd seen things he hadn't wanted her—or anyone—to see. And the edges of the neat and tidy box she'd put him in began to fray.

At the *thunk* of glass on wood Harper jumped.

Cormac had let his drink drop to the bar. Under his breath he said, "My mother is not a dark person. Circumstance played a part. Environment. Ill-fated choices."

Silence settled over them, as it was her turn to fill it. But there wasn't enough alcohol in the world to override her deeply ingrained aversion to getting personal. Harper's knee jiggled and she glanced back to the dance floor, figuring it the lesser of two evils.

Then Cormac sighed, used both hands to rub his face, before tugging them through his hair, leaving spikes in their wake. After pressing his fingers into his eye sockets, he once more looked out into nothing.

It had been a long time since a man had turned to her for solace. Either because she wasn't the kind of woman who attracted men who wore their hearts on their sleeve. Or because she'd avoided them at all costs.

Harper swallowed as a wave of regret broke over her. What if the son of the London restaurateur was right? Was she an empty, soulless, robot? Ice cool. Untouchable. Closed off to human emotion. Didn't the fact she kept half a world between herself and the person she loved most say it all?

Whether it was the rum—and bubbles and green stuff—speaking or if she'd truly had some sort of epiphany, Harper finished her iced water in one go, turned to Cormac, leaned her chin on her palm and said, "Tell me about it."

Cormac blinked several times then looked her way.

"Your mother," Harper said, forcing the words through numb lips. "Darkness. Ill-fated choices." She leaned in and gave Cormac a nudge with her shoulder. She'd sobered up enough to bounce back. "Think of me not as Harper Addison, Lola's dazzling big sister, but as a ghostly apparition, a stranger, a ship passing in the night. I'll be long gone by this time next week, so anything you say goes with me."

Cormac's gaze remained snagged on hers, thoughts too deep to catch slipping and shifting behind his corrupting eyes.

Then, with obvious effort, he dragged his gaze away, lifting his hand to call for another beer. Only when it was in front of him did he say, "That song."

"Which song?"

He tilted a chin towards the band. "The one you like so much. My father would play it *ad nauseam* the nights he was holed up in his study. I should like that song, as at least it meant there was a wall between him and my mother. And yet the warm, fuzzy feelings remain at bay." He lifted his drink to the heavens, as if offering a toast, then downed three large swallows.

"I'm taking it your dad was no peach."

Cormac coughed out a laugh, though he didn't look her way. As if imagining her a stranger was the only way he could get the words out at all. "Not so much. He was more of a mean bastard, actually."

Harper breathed, and forged on. "Did this have something to do with your mother's time in the dark?" A nod, then, "He blamed me for drawing her attentions away from him. He blamed her for my existence. He blamed us every chance he got."

He lifted his drink to his lips, then stopped. Put it slowly on the bar before pushing it away.

While Harper's throat tightened. Her insides twisting and squeezing. And it had nothing to do with the number of drinks she'd had.

She ached for all the things he hadn't said. The

confessions between the words. The grey area she usually had no time for. It was shaky ground for her. Terrifying, actually. But in her experience the only way out of the bad stuff was through.

"We, Lola and I, were brought up by our dad."

Cormac glanced her way, his eyes still warm, despite the subject matter. How did he do that? How did he keep his compassion when she had so little?

"Where was your mum?"

"She left. I was too young to really remember." Saying the words out loud, she felt like an overblown balloon. One slip and she'd burst. "But our dad, he was formidable."

Images of her father chased one another like drops of liquid mercury. "He'd take us out of school to spend entire days at the beach. He'd happily learn the dances we choreographed for him. Or wake us at midnight for chocolate feasts."

"Sounds like a hell of a guy."

"He was. Most of the time," Harper amended. "When he was on top. When things were bright and shiny. But when things got shaky, when things didn't go his way…"

The memories flipped over on themselves. "Like the time he came home with a litter of kittens, forgetting Lola was allergic. Or the times he forgot to pick us up from school at all."

"Was he violent?" Cormac asked, his voice rough.

Harper glanced over to find his attention completely hers, the man's charisma like a heat lamp, making her burn.

"Never that," she said. *Not, I imagine, like yours.* "He was…unreliable. Disorienting. Even during the good times, I felt as if I was walking on eggshells, always waiting for the ground beneath us to suddenly drop away."

Harper leant her elbows on the bar, and dropped her chin into her hands, her head suddenly too heavy for her neck to support.

Had she *really* felt that way? Even as a little kid? She must have. She'd simply never voiced it, as it would have made it real. It would have messed with the good memories of her dad she'd secretly let herself keep.

"I wonder now if there was something else there. Some undiagnosed condition. Bipolar perhaps? Something…"

She turned her head slowly, her brain following at a lapse. Saw Cormac watching her.

"I'm so sorry. We were talking about you, about *your* dad, and I totally hijacked things."

Cormac smiled, as if he too felt lighter than he had ten minutes earlier. As if talking to her had actually helped. "It's called a conversation, Harper. It's what grown-up people do whilst getting to know one another better."

"Is that what we're doing?"

"So it would seem."

Harper swallowed, trying to press down the uncomfortable feelings swelling inside her. And said, "Your dad—he was violent, wasn't he?"

Cormac picked up his beer, the bottle dangling between his fingers, the amber liquid swaying and sloshing against the glass. And after a beat he said, "He was an angry man."

"Why was he angry?"

"That I don't know. All I know is that he got off on making others feel insignificant. As if the only way he felt important was to make sure everyone else did not."

Harper remembered the conversation she'd had with Lola in the shop that morning. About how Cormac went out of his way to make sure everyone who worked for the Chadwicks feel as though they mattered. She'd seen herself that he'd done the same at school. And now she understood why.

He knew what it felt like to be marginalised. And, rather than give in, rather than believe it, he redressed the cosmic imbalance by making sure everyone else he ever met felt seen. Heard. Felt the glow of his attention.

She'd known he was special when she was a teenager. Now, having lived in the world, she knew how truly rare that quality was.

"I'm so sorry," she said. For his childhood. For thinking his motives were purely selfish. His closeness with the Chadwicks could not be put aside, but it was a strange kind of relief to know that he wasn't all bad.

"He died," Cormac said, without inflection. "Heart attack a number of years ago."

Harper nodded. "And your mum?"

"Has moved on admirably. She remarried a perfectly nice man with a bald patch and a caravan."

He pulled his phone out of his back pocket and slid it along the counter. Under a contact labelled "Mum", complete with a picture of an attractive woman with a short grey pixie haircut, was a message that had come through only a few minutes before.

Sorry, buddy, won't make it to Gray's wedding. Loving the reef so going to stay a while longer. Love, Mum. XXX

She glanced at Cormac to find him staring through the phone. "You were really hoping she'd come."

Cormac breathed out long and slow. "I was really hoping she'd come."

"How long has she been away?"

"A year. And a bit."

"She sounds like she's having a great time. Which is nice for her."

Cormac looked into the mouth of his near-full bottle, as though searching for an answer. He let out a sharp breath, as if he was letting something go. "I'm not sure why I even told you all that."

"Because I asked?"

He sniffed out a laugh. "Maybe."

In the onset of quiet, Harper heard the music had gentled. She glanced out towards the dance floor to see Lola and Gray slow dancing.

Wasn't that all anyone wanted in life? Someone who listened. Someone who stuck around.

Since the moment she'd looked into Cormac's eyes by the car outside the Chadwicks' house, there had been something there between them. She'd thought it the zing of latent attraction. Now she wondered if it went deeper. What if they'd recognised in one another the look of someone who had it all together, while inside they were both secretly hanging on by their fingernails?

Harper swallowed against the rising tide of something that felt a hell of a lot like tenderness and reached for her water.

"Way to bring the mood down, Wharton," she said, before having a gulp. "Just saying."

Cormac burst into laughter.

She caught his eye; saw light, brightness, oodles of charm. And her epiphany faded like mist on a morning lake. Either he actually *did* have it together, and tonight was a rare anomaly, or he was the best at hiding it she'd ever seen.

Either way the spell was broken. She couldn't

help but grin. Then soon joined in the laughing herself.

When they both settled down, Cormac asked the bartender to take away his untouched beer and ordered two more iced waters. Then they sank into an easy kind of quiet.

Until Cormac said, "You, Harper Addison, are an unexpected wonder and delight. When you're not all sniping and stubborn, that is."

His words whistled lightly through the air before lodging in her chest. "Well, you, Cormac Wharton, are far deeper than you at first appear."

Cormac coughed out one more laugh, taking the insult hidden inside the compliment for the mood-lightener that it was.

He held out his glass. She clinked hers against it.

And they drank.

Harper's heart felt strangely light. Lighter than she remembered it feeling in a very long time. Even as they sat close enough now that every time one of them breathed in, their arms brushed.

Yet neither made a move to pull away.

And, blinded by the light, she found herself saying, "So what do you really think of the happy couple? And this time I want the truth."

CHAPTER SIX

CORMAC GLANCED AT HER, then past her towards
the dance floor. Something flashed over his eyes.
A different kind of pain from the one he'd dealt
with earlier. For a second it felt like a mirror of
her own; that sense of missing something.

"Come on, Cormac," Harper pressed. Go hard
or go home. "Tell me what you really think about
Lola and Gray as a couple."

"I think they are madly in love."

"Do you?"

His eyes narrowed. "What's going on behind
those gorgeous yet devious eyes of yours now?"

Ignoring the "gorgeous" comment, or at least
tucking it away for later, Harper said, "Come on,
Cormac, you're a smart guy."

"Why, thank you."

She shot him a look. "You know Gray far better
than I do, so tell me if I'm wrong in thinking his
only ambition is finding the next wave."

Cormac did not tell her she was wrong.

"A man like that is not ready for marriage. For
forging a future. And what about fatherhood?
You can't seriously tell me you think this wedding ought to go ahead."

"I can," he said, lifting his water in salute. "And I will."

Then he let his glass drop as he looked deeper into her eyes. So deep she wondered if he might fall in.

Then he sat back far enough he had to grip the bar to keep his seat. He ran a hand through his hair, and Harper tried not to stare as it flopped back down into an adorable spiky mess. "You're serious."

"Of course I'm serious! This is my little sister. My flesh and blood. The only family I have left."

"What could you possibly have against Gray?"

"I don't have anything against him, *per se*." *His parents, on the other hand...* "Though for one thing, he's not the sharpest tool in the shed."

Cormac physically recoiled. Then looked off into the middle distance, muttering, "You're unbelievable."

"Lola is pure potential. She is far brighter than what she is currently doing. Which is my fault. I see that now. I gave her too much leeway. When she finally figures that out she'll regret this. She'll regret him."

Cormac shook his head.

"Then tell me what I'm missing. Convince me. Why should I think Gray is good enough for my sister?"

"Because he's Gray! Sure, he might appear a little laid-back. But so are half the guys who live around here. He might not be the most driven of all men, but he is all heart. Harper, he's a good man who adores your sister. What more could you possibly wish for?"

Harper breathed out hard. In a negotiation, when tempers were high, this would be the moment she tore the opposition's argument to pieces. But "good man" who "adored" her sister? The guy had just swept her legs out from under her.

Till Cormac added, "And Lola could not ask for better in-laws than Dee-Dee and Weston."

At that Harper snorted.

Dee-Dee seemed lovely. But Harper knew, she *knew*, what kind of man Weston Chadwick was. The depths he'd sink to in order to keep himself top dog.

Cormac did not appreciate her snort. She saw it in the cut of his shoulders. The sharpness of his gaze.

She wouldn't get any more insight out of him now. She'd drawn the lines and they stood firmly on either side.

She pushed her stool back.

Cormac twisted on his stool, blocking her. "Where are you going?"

"To the ladies' room. The dance floor. The other end of the bar. What does it matter?"

"Don't do anything stupid, Harper. Don't do anything you'll regret."

Harper's hackles rose into needle-sharp points.

When he breathed she felt it brush over her cheek and the rest of her woke as if dragged from a deep sleep.

His gaze shifted from one eye to the other. "What on earth could you possibly have against the *Chadwicks*?"

No. Not now. She had to talk to Lola about this first.

Cormac turned to look around the bar as if searching for reinforcements, and his knee knocked into hers before sliding past her thigh. Not that he seemed to notice.

Harper, on the other hand, noticed. Every inch of her that hadn't been touched felt cheated.

When his gaze once more found hers, he was close enough that she could feel his frustration. Like a heat wave washing over him, washing over her.

His voice was low, ruinous, as he said, "Tell me this: what does Lola have to offer the best friend I've ever had? The sweetest guy I've ever known? Apart from a bitter and confused sister she never sees and two MIA parents with murky pasts?"

He'd gone so deep, so fast, Harper blanched. For she felt herself flung back into the awful past couple of months at work, then right back to high school as if she'd been dragged there by icy claws.

"Wow," she managed, frantically trying to haul every self-protection measure she had back into place. "You really went there? Talk about going dark."

A muscle beneath Cormac's eye flickered, but she took little pleasure in the hit.

"Look, I have nothing to prove to you, Cormac. We don't need to be friends. The only thing I care about, the only thing in the entire world, is making sure my sister is happy."

Cormac lifted a hand to rub it over his face before glancing off to the side. "The worst part is, I think you actually believe it."

Harper reared back. "Excuse me?"

"If that's all you cared about, why have you been gone so long? If that's all you care about, why can't you simply be happy for her? Hell, if that's all you care about, why aren't you out there dancing with her while you have the chance? Why are you sitting here, jousting with me?"

While Harper mentally batted at his every accusation, Cormac laughed, the sound throaty and rich, but completely lacking in humour. Then he tipped forward, elbows on the bar, face landing in his palms. After a moment he gave his face a good rub before swinging his dark gaze back her way.

His hair was mussed, his eyes wild, and heaven help her she found herself so caught up in the heat of the man, she forgot for a second why he was looking at her that way.

Then he pushed to his feet and held out a staying hand. "Hang on a second. Could it be... Are you *jealous?*"

"What? No!" Harper took a deep breath. How had this turned so quickly? Persuading people to her way of thinking was her bread and butter. Why did Cormac Wharton have to be the one man who refused to drink the Kool Aid? "I'm not jealous. Not of them."

"Then what's the problem? Because I'm struggling to understand you, Harper. Try as I might. But every time I think I see a glimmer of humanity lurking beneath this slick, cool, ice-princess exterior you use as some kind of weapon and shield all wrapped up in one, the next second I wonder if I'm looking for something that just isn't there."

For all that his tone was even, his voice calm, his words hit Harper right at the heart of her.

Heartless. A robot. Out of touch with human emotion. Empty. Devoid. Not enough. Nothing at all.

Every bad thing she'd ever been called, every bad thing she'd ever feared about herself, every piece of her heart she'd closed in, tied off, cut away in order to protect herself, swam to the surface. And it was suddenly too much.

"Screw you," she said, pressing him back so she could get the hell out of there.

He opened his mouth to respond, but Harper

leaned in, pointing a finger in his face. "If you dare say *any time, anywhere*, I will hurt you."

Harper was too fired up to catalogue his tells, to decide if his slow breathing was a sign of him being in control, or fighting as hard as she was to find it.

Either way, she turned, shot a rather unladylike symbol over her shoulder and made to walk away.

But Cormac grabbed her by the arm. "Wait."

When she turned, glaring at where he held her, he eased off, but did not let go.

He swore beneath his breath. "You... I don't know why, but you drive me places I never go. Places no one else has come close..."

He took a deep breath and looked deeper into her eyes. "I'm sorry."

Harper braced herself as the backs of her eyes began to burn. "I don't care."

"You clearly do. Which proves my last statement wrong right there. Should never have said such a thing either way. Blame it on the beer, or the heat, or my mother's message, or that damn song. Or simply blame me."

Harper's lungs grew tight at the emotion in his words. At the wildness in his eyes. At the clutch in his voice as he said, "You do something to me, Harper."

Harper's knees gave way as if the ground beneath her feet had cracked.

Then he said, "You push my buttons in a way I can't explain."

When he saw he still had hold of her he let go as if burned, running his hand through his hair again.

You do something to me. How was she supposed to respond to that?

Her chest rose and fell. She could feel her blood racing beneath her skin. Hot and maddened.

"It's fine," she gritted out. "I mean, it's not fine. But whatever."

When he continued looking like a kicked puppy she slowly deflated, her anger leaving her in a trickle. It wasn't as if she'd been sweetness and light, after all.

She waved a hand his way, in a kind of blessing. "You're forgiven."

With a twitch at the corner of his mouth, Cormac bowed ever so slightly. But his voice was still raw as he said, "Why, thank you, milady."

When he straightened up she could have sworn he'd moved closer, for suddenly they were toe to toe. It would take nothing to lift a hand to his chest—that well-sculpted chest, with all that warm brown skin and its smattering of sun-kissed hair—to feel if his heart beat at anything like the pace hers did in that moment.

She watched, as if from a distance, as she did just that, her hand falling over his heart. She felt the throb, like a distant thud against her palm.

Then she felt it quicken. Beat harder. Reverberating through her palm until it might as well have been her pulse. Her heart.

"Harper," he said, his voice rough.

"Do I really do something to you?" She lifted her eyes to his.

Eyes that had gone so dark she couldn't tell the chocolate from the black.

"You really do."

From one heartbeat to the next, the hastily built wall she'd tried to construct between them fell away.

"Well, that's...nice."

He laughed, the sound rumbling from his chest to hers by some kind of sexual osmosis. "Harper, I can assure you, the last thing you make me feel is nice."

Right back at ya, she thought, paying hard attention to the conflict in his eyes. The same conflict she felt riding roughshod through her entire body.

She'd wanted to touch him so badly. Wanted him to touch her too.

She wanted to keep scrapping with him. And boy, did she want to run.

His hand lifted to brush the hunk of hair that had been bothering her behind her ear, and there it stayed. Big and warm and secure.

His thumb traced the edge of her face, his eyes

following the move. His chest rising and falling as he breathed deep.

She leant into his touch, just a little. Feeding on the unexpected tenderness like a woman starved.

When his eyes found hers, the blatant emotion therein made her ache all over.

But this was Cormac Wharton. He'd never looked at her, much less this way.

What if it was the beer? And the heat? And his mother's message? And the song? She began to wonder if she'd simply wandered into a perfect storm.

Until his gaze landed on her mouth.

The hunger in his eyes was unmistakable. Specific. Real.

She was in grave danger of sighing. In grave danger of crying.

"I'm going to kiss you now, Harper," he said, his voice ragged. "Just so you know."

There was time to pull a Harper and make light. It would allow her to save face. To keep her distance. To have the chance of getting through the rest of this week in one piece.

But this was Cormac Wharton. The boy who'd once held her heart.

The boy who'd broken it too.

No, she remembered as he shifted closer, as his spare hand stole around her back, as his hand delved deeper into her hair. As his body pressed up against her own, all muscle and heat.

This was no boy.

Cormac Wharton was all man.

Thank goodness, she thought as his lips closed over hers.

She'd imagined this moment more times than she could count. Imagined how he would taste, how he would feel. How she would feel.

As Cormac sipped on her mouth as if it was the sweetest thing he'd ever tasted she felt struck. Every cell jolting as one. Like lightning unable to find earth.

Cormac soon turned her to nothing but sensation. Heat. Pleasure. Somehow she found the wherewithal to slide a hand around his neck and another into his hair.

It was thick and soft and perfect.

Her lips opened on a groan. And Cormac took complete advantage, sliding his tongue over the seam of her lips, seducing them open. Not that he had to try too hard. She was all in.

Feeling it, Cormac hauled her closer, wrapping her up so tight she felt the evidence of exactly what she did to him.

Swamped by need and heat and desire so rich and warm, she felt it take her under, every thought dissolved into mist.

Until her leg wrapped around his, and her skirt pulled too tight against her thigh. While in a bar. In Blue Moon Bay.

Harper came back to reality with a thud.

Her eyes snapped open. She squinted against the brightness of the dome of light above the bar.

Cormac must have felt her freeze, as with one last kiss that made her insides go into free fall he pulled back. Looked into her eyes. And her heart squeezed so hard it hurt.

"Ow," she bit out.

And Cormac quickly stepped back, holding her lightly as if knowing exactly how boneless he'd left her.

"You okay?"

The only bit of her that hurt was the big, throbbing muscle behind her ribs, so she said nothing as she carefully extricated herself from his hands.

"Are you okay?" he asked again, and she shot him a look.

"Of course I'm okay."

Something acute flashed behind his eyes. "Okay."

"Just…" What? What could she possibly say? That she was shaken by how easily he'd taken her apart? That her whole body now ached for the lack of him? "Just, don't do that again."

A beat slunk by. His voice went deep as he said, "Which part exactly?"

"All of it."

"All of it? Right. Okay. You bet," he said, stepping away. Giving her space. Putting his hands in his pockets and leaning against the bar as if he hadn't a care in the world.

You bet? Really? As if it was nothing? As if he'd felt nothing? As if it meant nothing?

It had been as if he'd known her. Kissing not only with his mouth, but also with his touch, with his mind. She felt rearranged. As if her atoms were no longer where they had been before.

She wished she could simply turn and walk away, only her knees were no longer in optimal working order, so she had to regroup.

Harper stood tall, as tall as she could with the backs of her knees tingling like crazy and her heart threatening to beat right through her ribs. And she pointed a damning finger Cormac's way.

"You might be Gray's best man, and I might be Lola's maid of honour, but that does not mean we have to fall into some cliché by getting it on this week."

"Getting what on?"

"You know what I mean."

"I know that you kissed me."

"You kissed me!"

Cormac's smile said, *You know it. But you kissed me right on back, sweet cheeks.* He pressed away from the bar and took a step her way.

Harper's first instinct was to take a step back, knowing deep in her heart that, despite her demand not to kiss her again, if he came close enough for her to get even a whiff of his scent she'd be back to climbing him like a tree.

But her next instinct—her stronger instinct—

forged from necessity and experience, was to be strong.

For Harper never flinched. Even if it killed her.

So she stood her ground as Cormac crooned, "I've never been a best man before, so I'm not sure of the rules."

"There are no rules."

"Glad to hear it. Because that kiss has been coming for days."

Years, Harper thought, then bit her lip to stop that gem from spilling free.

"How about this, then: now that's out of our systems, let's agree to play nice for the rest of the week? I'll endeavour not to bite back if you push my buttons, while you can…"

Cormac waved a hand in front of her, as if incorporating every part of her in whatever it was she was doing wrong.

"So you'll try not to bite. While I'll try not to be quite so me."

He leant back and smiled, as if she had it in one. "Truce?"

Truce? Truce? The damnable man held out a hand. As if expecting her to shake it!

If it meant she could finally extricate herself from the hash she'd made of the evening, what the hell else could she do?

Harper grabbed his hand, shook it twice and blurted, "Now I'm going to dance. Out there."

"Go get 'em, tiger."

"I shall," Harper said, before turning on her heel and blindly disappearing into the crowd.

On the dance floor she found a spot on her own, closed her eyes and danced. Numb with the fact that fighting with Cormac was better than making love with any other man.

And if that wasn't the most messed-up thing she'd ever admitted to herself, she didn't know what was.

In the wee hours of the next morning, after the girls had wobbled into the Chadwicks' house together, Cormac whistled for Novak, who came bolting through the front doors of the manor before sticking to him like Velcro.

Only to find Gray leaning against the hood of the car.

His friend didn't waste any time getting to the point. "So you kissed her."

Dammit. "You saw that, huh?"

"You guys sucked up so much energy the lights flickered in the bar."

He'd have believed it too. For that kiss… Hell. He'd not meant to, even if he'd wanted to. He'd fought it, even as every word out of her mouth roused him. But the fever in her eyes, the way her breath caught whenever she found him watching her, the way she lifted her face to his, like a sunflower to the sun…

Cormac scratched the back of his neck. "Did Lola—?"

"Nah. I had her well distracted."

"Good." He opened up the car and Novak leapt in, taking up her usual spot on the back seat.

"Not so fast," said Gray, holding the door before Cormac could close it. "Wasn't it only a few hours ago you told me nothing was going to happen there?"

"Yeah."

"So, what happened?"

Cormac closed the door and leant against the car beside his oldest friend. "You want details? Need some pointers for your wedding night?"

Gray coughed out a laugh, before shooting Cormac a single hooked-eyebrow glare.

Cormac looked towards the house. Lights on in several rooms. Not Harper's; hers was around back. The fact he knew that spoke volumes as to the trouble he was in.

"She said stuff. Asked questions. Brought things to the surface. She talks. A lot. Only way I could think to shut her up."

"Fair enough," Gray shot back. "And if she says stuff again, talks too much again, what's the plan?"

"I think it's pretty clear there has not been a clear plan for me where Harper is concerned."

"You think? Look, you tell me it's just a best-man-maid-of-honour thing and I'll leave it well alone. More power to you both. We can look back on this in years to come and laugh and laugh. But if it's something that I need to worry about, something that might rebound onto my darling soon-to-be bride in *any* way, then I might have an opinion on the matter. Fair?"

Cormac hadn't been kidding when he'd said Gray was all heart. The guy rarely had strong opinions bar when to eat and who his people were. But when he did, he meant it.

Cormac nodded. "Fair."

Gray nodded back. Slapped his friend, hard, on the back and pressed away from the car. "All righty, then. See you at the lunch tomorrow?"

"Yeah, about that. I was hoping to beg off." A break from the partying, and from Harper, time to shake off the effect of her, would do him good. "I know your folks forbade me from going into the office this week, but they have an international business that needs running…"

Gray held up a hand as he backed away towards the house. "You are not sending me in there on my own, buddy boy. I will see you tomorrow at twelve. Don't be late."

"Aye-aye, Captain."

CHAPTER SEVEN

FORGOING A TRADITIONAL rehearsal dinner, the bride and groom had booked the entire *See Sure* restaurant for a family and friends lunch.

It had taken a shovel-load of concealer and mighty amounts of water to make Harper look and feel human after the night they'd had.

That, a killer navy halter dress held up behind the neck with a big satin bow, and her favourite fringed ankle-boot heels had her poised to meet Gray's mighty collection of guests, as well as Lola's far more meagre set, for a seafood buffet.

Harper had to admit a more stunning locale could not have been procured if she had been around to find one herself.

Abundant swathes of sheer white chiffon and tiny fairy lights were draped from the moulded ceiling, leaving glimpses of whitewashed walls. Small bowls of lush succulents had been scattered down the long table, while white and gold place settings glinted and sparkled in front of the fifty-odd rustic wooden chairs.

It was fresh and casual, with glints of sophistication. It was Lola. Not Lola of the yoga pants and baseball caps, but exactly as Harper saw her.

Someone else had done this for her. Someone else who knew Lola that well.

Harper had been struggling since she'd arrived, owing to a sense of inevitability as the days rolled forward until Lola would no longer belong only to her.

Only, looking around at the smiling faces of those Lola deemed close, Harper realised that moment had long since passed.

Harper could live with that, so long as she knew for sure that this was the best possible path for Lola's future.

Today, her focus would remain sharp. If Lola showed even the slightest tell that she was anxious—twitchy gaze, tight voice, fingers tripping over one another as a way to disperse excess nervous energy—she'd instantly find a way to tell her the truth about the Chadwicks. And about their father's last days at home.

Harper kept her radar on as she met Lola's yoga friends—high on holistic health and Instafit likes—as well a couple of Lola's mates from her incomplete university degree.

The rest of the women at the table were already familiar to her. There was maudlin Marcy, ditsy Dana and sly Serena—the *über*-rich girls of Blue Moon Bay High and members of Gray and Cormac's high-school clique.

No tenacious Tara, though, Harper noted. Interesting. Except, *not*. What did it matter to Harper if

Cormac and his high-school girlfriend were still tight or not? Not a jot!

As for Cormac, he sat sideways on his chair at the other end of the table, cradling a coffee rather than a beer, as if he too was doing what had to be done to recover from the night before. He listened intently as the guy beside him told a story, suit jacket over a dark T doing him all sorts of favours.

Not that she was watching him. Or constantly reliving that kiss. Or wondering if he was too.

Harper turned in her seat as a woman plonked herself into the chair beside her. *Adele*, Harper thought, quickly glancing across the table at Lola. Was this the sign she'd been looking for that things weren't as they appeared?

For Adele had been Queen Bee of Blue Moon Bay High. And Gray's high-school girlfriend. Now she was leaning over the table to touch hands with Gray's mother, blowing air kisses to Gray's father.

"Harper," said Lola. "You remember Adele."

Adele stopped shuffling in the seat and gave Harper a quick once-over.

Adele held out a hand, which Harper shook. "The pleasure is all mine."

"Adele's family owns this joint," Lola said. "When she offered it up for the day we couldn't have been happier. Right, honey?"

Gray looked up at Lola's voice and smiled.

"Wedding gift sorted," said Adele with a wave

of her hand. Then she turned on her chair, her knee bumping Harper's. "Harper Addison. What's your story? Where did you disappear to after the hell that was high school?"

Harper looked at Adele again, to find no irony on her face. Just open interest.

"I'm a freelance corporate negotiator," she said, "based out of Dubai."

Adele nodded. "Dubai, I know. The rest went right over my head."

"She flies all over the world," said Lola, her voice carrying so that others listened in, pride tinging every word, "to sort out corporate squabbles, messy mergers and contract negotiations. Think Fortune 500 companies, even governments. They bring in my big sister when things go really sour. She's the last word."

"So, you're a total badass. In heels."

For all that Harper tried to dislike Adele, she failed. "Damn straight. Though most of the time it's less Wild West and more like being a stern kindergarten teacher, only the students are stubborn fifty-year-old millionaires."

"Huh," Adele said. "And did you look like this in high school?"

"Same bones. Less gloss."

"I hear that. Were you one of Gray's swooning acolytes, by any chance?"

Harper looked to Lola and said, "No. Never."

Lola shrugged. "I wouldn't blame you if you

were. He was hot stuff in high school. So many of my friends had crushes on Gray."

"And yet I was not one of them," Harper insisted, realising how much of the table was now looking their way.

Even Gray, who gave her a wink. A wave of his hand. *All good.*

While Adele was not to be deterred. "If not Gray, who was your high-school crush?"

Harper should have seen it coming. But after the hot days and long, restless nights she was off her game. She didn't even feel herself turn towards Cormac until it was too late.

Her eyes brushed over him for a heartbeat. Maybe less. But it was enough, and in case anyone at the table missed it Adele lifted a hand and pointed a finger Cormac's way.

Harper's gaze flicked back to Lola in time to see her eyes widen. As if all her Christmases had come at once.

Then Harper caught Adele's eye and shook her head. Just once.

A flicker of understanding warmed Adele's eyes, before she clapped her hands and shouted, "Okay, kids, enough of the polite wine. Shots all round!"

A bevy of nattily dressed waiters brought trays covered in an array of fierce-looking shots and conversation once more filled the room with its warm buzz as Harper's moment in the spotlight was fast forgotten.

Lola grabbed a shot, downed it fast, then stood and said, "Wee time," to no one in particular.

Harper was on her feet in an instant, the loud scrape of her chair sending curious gazes her way. She offered a tight smile to the table at large, her own gaze snagging on Cormac, who now watched her in that warm, intense way of his.

Had he seen? Had he heard?

She shook her head, shook him off and followed her sister to the bathroom.

"Lolly?"

"Harps!" Lola said on a sigh. "Isn't this the best day ever? I'm so happy you're here. So happy everyone is here."

"Everyone?"

The toilet flushed and Lola stumbled out. "Of course!"

When Lola waved her hands under the tap and nothing happened, Harper turned it on for her. And asked, "Even Adele?"

"Especially Adele. She's the best. She knows everybody. She put me on to the cake lady. Told me the name of this amazing guy who custom-makes wedding rings. She even manages the band who are playing at the reception. Such a cool chick, don't you think?"

"That she is." How to put this? "It doesn't bother you that she and Gray used to…"

Lola blinked. Then burst out laughing. "That was ages ago. Besides, Adele is gay! Or bi, I guess, if you take the Gray anomaly into account."

"Right." She had wondered, what with Adele looking at her as if she was lunch.

"Adele got Gray through Chemistry and he got her through teenagerhood with uptight, unforgiving parents. From the look of things, she's quite taken with you. If you're keen." Lola waggled her eyebrows.

Harper levelled her with a look.

"Well, how am I supposed to know? I haven't seen you in years. And you never talk about the men in your life. You could be gay, or married with seven kids, for all I know."

Harper didn't realise she was holding her breath until her throat felt uncomfortably tight.

She moved to take Lola by both hands. "I'm not gay, honey. Or married with seven kids. Or seeing anyone right now. But when I do see people they are men. And if you have any other questions about me, about my life, ask away."

A smile tugged at the corners of Lola's mouth. "Did you seriously have a crush on *Cormac* in high school?"

Harper's instinct was to deny, deny, deny. But this was Lola. She'd made the decision to be honest with her little sister about their past, meaning she had nowhere to hide.

Quickly checking to make sure the other stalls were empty, Harper said, "Yes."

"That's awesome! Did you write his name all over your school books?"

Harper's eyes closed in mortification. "Yes. I imagined what our kids would look like. The whole gamut."

Lola shot her a sly look. "So what about now? Crush still alive and kicking?"

Harper shook her head, no. For what she felt for Cormac was nothing so plain and simple as a crush. It was far more complicated in the way adult things tended to be.

"But he's so hot," Lola encouraged.

"Lola, come on."

"Watching him surf is one of life's great pleasures, don't you agree? And he's funny too. Dry. And seriously smart. Loyal. Sweet as pie. According to the Chadwicks, he's a lifesaver. I've heard them say more than once that they owe their current success to him and only him."

Harper channelled Teflon, allowing Lola's words to roll off her back.

"If you need for me to put in a good word, let Cormac know you're available, I will."

"Please don't."

"Are you sure? Because I really wish I could see you as happy as I am."

Lola's words, and the truth of them in her eyes, hit Harper like a harpoon, right through the belly.

Was Lola happy? How could she really know for sure? Her world was so limited. Harper should have encouraged her to travel more, before she met Gray. She should have taken Lola with her…

This time Lola took Harper by the hands. "Are you happy, Harps?"

"If you're happy, then I'm happy," said Harper, using the same mantra she'd used on Lola for the past decade. "It's that simple."

And it had been that simple. It really had. It had kept Harper going when it had all seemed too hard. When she'd doubted. When she'd failed.

Only now she was here, back in this place, seeing Lola not as the needy teenager, but as a woman who had moved on, made decisions, made friends, made plans, put down roots, fallen in love—she should have felt triumphant.

And yet Harper felt…lost.

For what had Harper done in the same time?

Worked. Worked. And worked some more.

She had money, she had respect, she had a closet full of fabulous clothes.

But she had no people in her life. No roots. She had no plans bar the next couple of contracts. She'd spent more time in the past two years to London and back than she did in her own apartment which was really nothing more than a place to keep her dry cleaning.

"Okay, then," Lola said as she fixed her ponytail in the mirror. "Ready?"

For what? Harper nearly asked. Going back out there with those girls who'd never looked twice at her in high school? With the man who'd ruined her father's life? With the boy who'd twisted her heart in his fist, who had become the man who was fast making inroads in that same direction yet again?

Not even close.

But Harper was good at putting on a brave face. Always had been. Always would be. "Let's do this!" she said.

Then Lola took her by the hand and led her back out into the big, bad world.

The hens' night and bucks' party turned out to be a joint affair.

With the older generation saying their goodbyes around five, the lights in the See Sure faded, a disco ball dropped from the ceiling, the wait staff cleared away the tables and a dance floor and DJ appeared as if from nowhere.

Trays of jelly shots did the rounds. Someone handed out wigs, novelty headbands. A face-paint artist painted tattoos onto arms, butterflies onto faces, even six-packs onto less-than-toned bellies.

Harper danced just enough to keep Lola off her case, but drank nothing but water. She made sure to eat whenever a tray of nibbles came around. And she kept herself alert. Frosty. All the better to avoid any more accidental revelations of any kind.

And somehow, she managed to avoid Cormac all night long.

Until Lola bundled her up to an old-fashioned photo booth, right as Gray made his way out.

"Your turn!" Lola said, forcing Harper inside.

Harper flapped the dusty red curtains away from her face as she stumbled inside. Only to find Cormac already there, making to stand. When he looked up and spotted her, he stopped; knees bent, hands glued to his thighs, too tall to fit in the booth upright.

"Hi," he said.

Panicked, she tried to back out, but someone's hands—Lola's, no doubt—grabbed her backside and gave her a shove.

Meaning it was either stumble onto the small bench seat beside Cormac or end up splayed against him like a starfish. She chose the seat.

After a mortifyingly long wait, Cormac did the same.

She shuffled over. Made room.

Not enough though. With nowhere to put his long legs, he settled his thigh against hers, sending little shock waves up and down her side.

"So now what?" she muttered.

"It takes a few minutes to warm up. A red light comes on. And then we smile. Easy."

Harper looked around the room, feigning interest in the dark glass behind which the camera no doubt resided. In the seventies wood panelling on the walls. In the strips of photos, showcasing all the different kinds of faces one might care to pull.

"Having a good time?" Cormac asked.

"Hmm?" said Harper, turning to Cormac as if she only just remembered he was there.

His eyes smiled a half-second before his lips did the same. "Are you having a good time?"

"Sure. You?"

His pause was telling. As was the deep breath in, and heavy breath out. When, rather than answer, his gaze travelled away from her eyes, tracing her face, he might as well have said out loud that none of it mattered to him. Until now.

You do something to me, Harper.

Everything had shifted off its axis when he'd said those words to her the night before. Sitting there next to him in the quiet of the booth, the sounds of the party roaring like a storm outside, there was no denying he'd done something to her too.

Not only on that fateful day in high school, when his words had forged the backbone that had put her in good stead through her twenties. But this week. He was doing something to her right now, just by sitting there.

When her eyes meandered back to his it was to find him watching her, smiling as if he'd been watching her watch him for some time.

She swallowed. "How many minutes does it take to warm up?"

"Some," he said, his throaty voice filling the booth.

Harper wriggled on the seat, though it only served to rub her up against him all the more.

"Am I the only one who feels like I'm back in high school? Forced into a closet for a game of five minutes in heaven?"

He said nothing to that, merely stared at her as shadows of smoke swirled into his eyes. "I never played. Did you?"

"Once. Tenth grade. Samuel Clifford's party."

"Who did you end up in the closet with?"

"Samuel. Everyone ended up in the closet with Samuel."

Cormac threw back his head and laughed, the deep sound reverberating in the small space before bouncing about behind her ribs.

"And this feels like *that*?"

"It feels like something," she murmured. She leant forward, squinted at the tiny array of instructions. "Nothing will happen unless we press that button."

"You don't say."

"Hang on, you knew that because you've done this already."

"While you've been flitting around like a hummingbird all night, doing everything in your power to avoid me." Frown lines creasing above his nose, he turned his big body towards her, his leg brushing slowly against hers. "If you don't want to be here, Harper, all you have to do is open up the curtain and go."

She looked towards the curtain—red velvet, pocked with moth bites—heard the murmur of voices, music, laughter outside.

For all her bravado, and talk of preferring big cities with plenty on offer, she was an introvert at heart. Far happier to sit up in bed on a Saturday night with a juicy corporate report than partake in the nightlife of whichever city she was in. No chance of making friends that way. No chance of losing them either.

Then there was the fact that Cormac was beside her. All warm, and big, and combative.

Her toes curled in her shoes. And she stayed.

"Mmm…" Cormac rumbled. "That's what I thought."

She shot him a glance out of the corner of her eye. "I'm just taking a moment. It has nothing to do with you."

"Of course. I'd never have dared suggest you prefer my company above all others'. Consider me put in my place."

Harper opened her mouth to soften her statement, before figuring she'd only dig herself a bigger hole.

After a couple of long, interminable beats of silence, Cormac said, "Nothing wrong with taking a moment."

"I know."

"Nothing wrong with showing concern for your sister."

She shot him a look, saw it filled with understanding and insight into how things had unfolded between them the night before.

"Nothing wrong with feeling vulnerable either. Or tired. Or fed up. Or nervous. Or out of place. Or scared."

"I know that too," she lied. How could she convince others she was bulletproof if she couldn't convince herself?

"Then, why pretend?"

"Pretend what exactly?"

"To have it all so under control."

"Who says I don't?"

He shot her a look. As if he knew her. Understood her. As if he cared.

"I'm talking about the heels, the hair, the matching bling." He reached up as if about to run a curl through his fingers before letting his hand drop. "Being so together at work is one thing. It no doubt requires for you to appear in command. But nobody can be expected to be this perfect all the time."

Harper blinked. Her gaze catching on his as he finished a slow, meandering mapping of her face. How did he do that? Was she really that transparent? Or only to him? And had Cormac Wharton just called her perfect?

She *knew* better than anyone she wasn't that.

Though for her entire childhood she'd tried to be the "perfect" daughter. Her grades had been impeccable, the house always pristine. She'd won awards for math, debating, her charity fundraising. Even her lemon yoghurt cake at the town fair. Because she'd known, deep in her heart, that her father was hanging on by his fingernails too.

Clearly it hadn't been enough.

She glanced down at her hand to find she'd been picking at the edge of a fingernail, chipping the glossy black polish away, something she hadn't done since she was a kid. And said, "I'm far from perfect, Cormac."

"I'm well aware."

"Wow. You didn't even have to think about it."

His grin was fast, a flash of humour and heat. And in the small, enclosed space Harper felt as if her heart had grown a size too large.

"Nobody is," Cormac said. "We are all slovenly, frustrated, confused animals, trying to be civilised. And that's okay. It's the fact that we try to be better, that we learn from our mistakes, that moves us up the evolutionary scale. We are a lot—the people in this place. So if you're tired, if you've had enough of us, tell us so. Or go grab a patch of quiet. The Chadwick grounds are vast. Plenty of places to get lost."

Harper's instinct was to sit tall, to deny that she had a clue as to what he was talking about. But in the protection of their little booth she let out a large, exhausted sigh. "Thanks. I'll do that."

His next smile was smaller, less flash, and yet it hit deeper. Warming her from the inside out.

"So, I have news," he said.

"Such as?"

"You had a crush on me in high school."

Harper froze.

"When Amy heard Adele she told Tad, who told Weston, who told me. I figured it was nothing more than Chinese whispers but by the look on your face... Wow. It's true."

Realising she'd just given herself away, Harper only groaned louder.

The entire booth shook as Cormac sat back in the seat. Harper's gaze crept sideways to find him sitting with his head against the wall, looking at the ceiling.

"How did I not know this?" he asked.

"Nobody knew! Okay, so people probably knew. But everyone was too scared to call me on it. You probably don't remember, because it's now clear you had no idea who I was, but I was a bit scary in high school."

His head tipped sideways, until Harper found herself tangled in those intense dark eyes. Then his gaze narrowed as it moved to her hair, her cheeks, her mouth.

"I remember darker hair, wild curls. Doc Marten boots. Flyers and demands for action. And you were one of those really smart kids, the extension kids, right? Were you even in my biology class once?"

Harper scrunched up her face. "Yeah, that pretty much covers it. While you…"

She couldn't help herself—her gaze travelled over his face, cataloguing the changes in him: the firm jaw, the lines at the corners of his eyes, the scar cutting through his right eyebrow. Before also finding all the things that had drawn her to him in the first place—the smiling mouth, the size of him, as if he could protect the world, and those warm, magnetic eyes.

"You were like this handsome prince. Your whole gang always laughing and leaning all over one another, ruling the school. It was pretty seductive for a serious loner like me."

Cormac's gaze hardened for a fraction of a second. "I was lucky to have them. But you know we weren't all that we seemed."

She did. Now. But those memories were hard to budge.

"Anyway, back to that crush of yours—"

"No. Uh-uh. That subject is closed. It was many years ago when I was young and stupid."

"I can't imagine you were ever all that young. Or stupid for that matter. Hang on, I remember a speech. Wasn't that you who accused the school board of fascism because of the sexist uniform policy?"

"Yep. That was me. I was quite the little radical." Her dad had loved it. Loved her sticking it to the man.

Ironic that after he'd left it had been those radical instincts that had saved her; in scrapping, in fighting, in keeping a low profile so that Lola wasn't taken away from her.

Harper wondered what else he might soon remember. Such as the last thing he'd ever said to her before leaving school. When he'd dismissed her so wholly, as if she was no more than a fly buzzing by his ear.

She dared not ask. Not when his eyes dropped to her mouth and made her feel anything but irrelevant.

"So, are we going to do this?" he asked, his deep voice curling beneath her defences.

Harper's gaze dropped to his mouth too and she remembered how it had felt on hers. She wanted to. God how she wanted to. But if there was ever a time when she needed to see the world in black and white, this was it.

"I'm not sure that I can."

"We are making up our own rules, remember?"

"Then my number one rule is to not do anything I'll soon regret."

"What's to regret? You have a thing against devastatingly handsome lawyers?"

"I have a thing against devastatingly handsome lawyers with dibs on themselves."

"So, you do think I'm handsome. Knew it!"

He punched the air like a jock after a touchdown and Harper couldn't help but laugh. Then she said, "Let me put it this way: Lola. Gray. Enough said."

His voice dropped as he said, "Did it not occur to you that Lola and Gray conspired to get us in here together?"

Harper opened her mouth to deny him then thought about how Gray had come out of the booth right as Lola had shoved her in. "It's more complicated than that."

"How?"

"I…can't."

"You…won't. It's not the same thing. Huh."

"What?"

"I never would have thought of you as a coward, but here we are."

Harper knew he was goading her. Calling her chicken in order for her to bite back and give him what he wanted. But this wasn't school. Thank goodness.

She was a grown woman.

And he was all man. God, the scent of him filling the cramped cubicle was like fresh laundry and sunshine, with an undercurrent of male desire.

She didn't realise she'd been staring at him, while nibbling at the inside of her bottom lip, until Cormac's gaze darkened, nostrils flaring, throat working.

Then he said, "Just so we're clear, when I said, 'Are we going to do this?' I meant, 'Are we going to take the photos?'"

"You did not."

A smile spread slowly over Cormac's mouth. Then he leant over to touch the magic button. On the machine. Not her magic button. That would have been—

Harper shook her head as a wave of sensation rushed over her, threatening to make her swoon.

The machine began to whir as it warmed up, loaded the film, or whatever it did to ready itself.

"I never knew you enough to give you a lock of hair, so we'll get you your keepsake today," Cormac said. "Every girl with a crush deserves one—it's the least I can do."

"Seriously—"

A flash went off, filling the small box with light and—

Click.

"What? Was that a photo?" Of her gawping at Cormac while he smiled gorgeously towards the lens?

"Next one's only a few seconds away," he warned, shuffling to put his arm around her.

"I can't believe I'm doing this," she muttered as she tucked herself into his side. The heat of him washed over her, his scent filling her lungs. She puffed out a breath between pursed lips and—

Click.

"I wasn't ready!" she cried.

"Just sit still and smile."

"Okay."

At the last second, he turned and kissed her on the cheek.

Click.

"Cormac!"

She turned to chastise him, only to find him so close they bumped noses. She froze. He nudged her nose once more, this time with purpose.

Then he leaned in and kissed her, this time pressing his lips gently, so gently, against her lips.

And whatever she'd been about to say slipped right out of her head as sweet, painful longing overtook every other feeling.

Click.

Harper's eyes flickered open, slowly, unsurely. To find Cormac on his feet and sweeping the velvet curtain aside.

While Harper couldn't move. The sounds of the party slowly came back to her—laughter, music, chatter. The ground beneath her feet felt unstable, as if it was tipping and swaying. As if she didn't know which way was left any more. Which way right.

Things didn't just happen to Harper, not any more. She'd made sure of it. She was her own boss. She took on the jobs she wanted to take on. She had no problem with saying no. She was in charge of her destiny.

But this place was undoing her. This man… He worried she wouldn't let herself feel vulnerable. Nervous. Scared. With him that was *all* she felt.

If she didn't get a handle on things and soon, she feared she might never quite get a hold of the strong, grounded, serious parts of herself again.

It was time to take back control.

She reached up and grabbed Cormac's hand. He stopped, looked back at her, eyes questioning.

"You want to get out of here?"

He didn't even hesitate, didn't draw breath as he said, "Hell, yeah."

CHAPTER EIGHT

DESPITE THE WARM summer weather, they were about as close as one could get to Antarctica while still remaining on mainland Australia, meaning a crisp chill had well and truly fallen over Blue Moon Bay.

Cormac changed down a gear as they neared the coastal road gouged into the cliff-side.

Beside him Harper pulled up the collar of the jacket he'd insisted she borrow, and leant back against the headrest, watching the sky. He snuck a glance before the road became too precarious. Drank in her hooded eyes, long, tip-tilted nose and those tempting full lips.

He knew how soft those lips were. He knew the taste of them, the heat. He knew the sounds that came from them as she melted in his arms.

She folded her arms over her chest and sighed.

"Don't get stars like this where you live," Cormac said.

"We get great stars. Have you been to Dubai?"

"Stopover only." He couldn't remember on the way to where. Once he'd left home at eighteen, with only days to go before he finished high school, he hadn't stopped there. Studying abroad, and working all hours so he could see the world.

So he could keep moving. So he didn't have to look back.

"Did you never think about staying in the States?" she asked. "Or England? London could well be my favourite city."

Cormac swallowed. It had been his too. "I'm pretty sure we've covered this ground already."

She waved a hand his way. "That was before."

Before what exactly? Before they'd taken off in his car after disappearing from a party they should not have disappeared from. Before they'd kissed. Before they'd begun to find ways to be together as much as humanly possible.

"What is the answer you're looking for, Harper?"

She breathed out, long and loud, and said, "I don't know."

Excellent. Then they were both on the same page. Because he had no clue what he was doing here either.

Leaving Gray's bucks' night without saying a word was not like him at all. He'd spent his adult life taking pains never to put his own needs over the needs of others in an effort to make sure he never even came close to becoming his father.

Now he was in the car with no idea as to where they might end up.

Then, like a little gift, he saw a familiar turn in the road.

He slowed, shifted down a gear. The low-slung chassis juddered as they edged onto the dirt road and curled their way up the hill. Peering through the darkness, he found the two painted posts that pointed the way to the spot he was looking for.

The shale crackled under his tyres as he slowed to a halt just before the land dropped away once more, and the lights of the town shimmered down below.

"Where are we?' Harper asked. Then she sat bolt upright, his jacket falling a little off one creamy shoulder before she hooked it back into place. "You're kidding me, right?"

"What?"

"This place. This is…" Her voice lowered as she said, "Kissing Point."

He leaned a mite towards her, his voice dropping to match. "And we're the only ones here. So why are we whispering?"

She looked around, and sat back in her seat. "How many girls you must have brought up here."

"Just one, mainly."

"Right. Tara Parker."

Cormac's mouth twitched. He'd taken the "high-school crush" thing with a grain of salt. But all these years later she remembered the name of his senior girlfriend? Well, what do you know?

Deciding to see how deep it went, he lay back

against the headrest and said, "Ah, Tara. Oh, how you brought happiness and light to a young man's life."

Harper's look was blistering. "Wow. Heartfelt. Are you still in touch?"

Cormac turned a little to face her, his knee bumping hers. She noticed. Eyes widening. Breath hitching. But she didn't shift away.

"We are," he said. "Social media. We occasionally bump into one another at the supermarket, or a party every now and then. She married Josh Cantrell."

Harper's nose twitched. Not a Josh fan, then. Cormac didn't blame her. The guy was a douche.

"They have four sons under the age of five."

"Four? Good lord."

"Amen." Then, "You really want to know why I came home?"

"Yeah," she said, "I really do."

He considered his words. Considered making a joke, which was often his way when things edged towards tension.

In the end he went with the truth. "I had an epiphany."

"Did you just?"

"Oh, yeah. A big one. The kind that smacks you across the back of your head so hard you see stars. I figured out the meaning of life."

"Wow. So it was a *big* epiphany."

"The biggest."

"Care to share?"

"The meaning of life? Sure. It's about figuring out what makes you happy and doing more of that."

He waited for Harper's zinger, for offering such an idealistic notion was sure to invite derision. But it never came. Instead she watched him with those quixotic hazel eyes of hers.

Then she lifted a hand to swipe a lock of hair from her cheek. A shaking hand. And he wished he knew what the hell he'd said. Something that had made it past that big, thick wall of self-protection she wore like a walking safe room.

Yet he was well aware of how she reacted when pushed, so he let it be, looking out across the lights of Blue Moon Bay instead.

Keeping his voice light, he said, "For me that means surfing. This glorious old car. Old movies. True friends." He paused, holding the last on the list on the back of his tongue, as it had always felt like a private need, a secret too close to home, before he felt as if she needed to know it, more than he needed to hold it in. "It also means doing good work, for good people, that makes me feel of use."

He spared a glance for Harper, to find her looking out across the town. "What makes you happy, Harper?"

She breathed in deep, breathed out hard. For a moment he thought she was too caught up in her thoughts to have heard him, before her brow furrowed and she said, "Money in the bank. Mostly for the freedom it brings with it, but also the ability to buy shoes without checking the price."

"I hear that."

She lowered her eyes as a smile flashed across her face. Then added, "I love crisp, clean sheets. Room service. A long, hot shower under a showerhead with oomph." Cormac turned to face her a little more. Watching her eyes as she spoke; her cheekbones—the kind Hitchcock would have killed to light; the curve of a mouth built to drive a man out of his mind.

She turned to face him too, her eyes lit with an inner fire as she said, "I love standing in front of a boardroom filled with suits and knowing that I'm in control. That I am there because those smart, powerful, lauded people caused a right mess, and I'm the only one who can fix it. And when all's said and done they legally agree to follow my recommendations and do as I say."

That he did not doubt for a second.

"But it's not about the power trip. It's about making things right. About turning what has become an explosive situation that could break people into a fair, thoughtful compromise in which nobody loses their house."

Cormac's next breath out was tough.

She presented to the world like a professional ball breaker, but he'd known she was more. He wouldn't have been so drawn to her if beneath the implacable exterior he hadn't been able to sense her big heart.

But, he wanted to know, did any of those things make her *happy*?

Her voice seemed far away as she said, "But you know what?"

"What?"

"I would gladly give all of that away if that's what it took to make sure Lola was happy."

"She is."

She swallowed, her throat working as she said, "So it would seem."

"So what will you do now? Where does all that fierce focus of yours go?"

She opened her mouth and shut it again, doing a fine impression of a fish out of water.

"More long, hot showers, perhaps? More time to squish suits under the heels of your expensive shoes?"

Her mouth tightened, her focus coming back on line. "Like you can talk."

"What does that mean?"

Her chin rose, heat swirling behind her sultry hazel eyes, as she said, "What is it you do exactly? I mean, from what I've seen you surf, you chat up the customers and you drive people around. But there has to be more."

Cormac laughed, the sound coiling deep inside of him and holding on tight. He was a smart man. He knew how she reacted any time they came anywhere close to intimacy. She was baiting him to keep him at arm's length.

Hell, he'd just admitted to himself that he did the same thing, only he used humour to keep anything too close to real conversation at bay.

This push-pull dynamic was completely new to him. She was abrasive, stubborn, and she made him itch, but the attraction was undeniable. Damn scary, in fact, how fast it had come on. How deep it already went. Especially when he still wasn't all that sure he trusted her.

By this point he was acting on gut instinct alone.

The same instinct that had him saying, "The Chadwick companies are more than just a clothing brand. We are sports equipment designers. We own manufacturing plants, real estate, restaurants, shipping and logistics businesses as well as many other concerns. We work hard to put as much business back into the region as we can, in order to keep the local economy booming, but we also build and serve every community in which we run. We employ thousands of workers across the globe. All our products are made using adult labour with fair pay. We run more than one charity under the Chadwick umbrella—medical research, domestic violence shelters, educational scholarships—with ninety per cent of all monies raised going direct to the beneficiaries. And of all that I am lead counsel."

He turned to Harper to find her watching him, eyes wide and gleaming in the moonlight. No wonder. His words had scattered like artillery fire, ready to take out anyone who dared deny the veracity of his speech.

"You want to know what I do, Harper? While—after years spent keeping this entire town afloat—the Chadwicks finally get to enjoy their well-earned retirement, and Gray—my big, kind, sweet, loving best mate—enjoys the hell out of his blessed life like the trust-fund kid that he is, I run the damn lot."

"Cormac, I didn't mean—"

"Yes, you did."

Cormac ran a rough hand through his hair.

What the hell was it about her that made him feel the need to prove himself? To make her believe that he was content, settled and damn well happy? When deep down she made him feel it was time to shed his skin.

If only he could get her out of his head. If only he could keep his eyes off her. Stop touching her whenever the chance arose, as if making sure she was still there. If only he could pinpoint what it was about her that had swept him up so fast, so hard.

Then maybe he could figure out which parts of him she'd left untouched, untattered, unchanged, and he could rebuild from there. He'd done it before when he'd been nothing but a shell of a boy. He could do it again.

"Look," he said, doing his all to gentle his voice, "I've tried to be pleasant. Tried to be welcoming. Tried to be accommodating for your sister's sake, for the sake of the Chadwicks. But enough is enough, Harper. You've had it in for me from the moment you arrived. What I want to know is why."

He could all but see the invisible quills popping up all over her skin. Protective measures locking into place. Then, before he even felt her move, she was outside, the car rocking as she slammed the door behind her.

She turned only to toss his jacket into the back seat, as if shedding him as well, before she paced to the front of the car.

Her silhouette cut into his view. Moonlight poured over her bare shoulders, glinting off the silken sheen of a dress that hugged her curves like a second skin, turned her movie-siren hair to silver.

The air around her shimmered with her intense energy. He'd never met anyone who held on as tight. Who was as impossible to crack. So why the hell did he keep trying?

He gripped the steering wheel as too many emotions to count slammed over him like a series of rogue waves. Went to slam his wrists against it, before stopping himself at the last. Breathing. Temper gentling.

He kept trying because, while he might not yet trust her, he trusted himself. His instincts were decent. His motives genuine. He would not have been so drawn to her without good reason.

Cormac alighted from the car, shut the door carefully, walked to her, before hitching himself up onto the tough old bonnet.

When she finally turned, levelling him with a look, he patted the spot next to him.

As he'd known she would she held out a beat, before leaning back against the bonnet next to him. Because, strange as it was for such a short acquaintance, he felt as though he *knew* her. And, knowing her, he only wanted to know more.

The breeze rustled her hair, sending a waft of her heady scent his way.

"Harper, I need you to talk to me. Did Lola tell you something about me that doesn't sit right? Is it something to do with my father? Did you know him back then?" Not that, please let it not be that. "Or was it something at school? Did I not take your causes seriously? Did I hurt your feelings in some way?"

There. The brisk lift of her shoulders. Harper said nothing, her face a case study in elusive shadows, but with a sinking feeling in his chest Cormac realised that while trying to make light he'd somehow hit the mark.

What the hell had he done? His last couple of years of school were a blur in his memory. A haze. While things had spiraled out of control at home, he'd become cocooned in his group of friends.

Never before had he wished he could remember it all. He'd blocked it out deliberately; the shouting, the fights, the bruises, the terror that this time might be the last. The feeling that his soul was trying to burst out of his skin. He knew he'd growled at poor kids who got in his way. Stopped listening when a friend was telling a story. He'd skipped school. Stolen beer. Drunk it while skipping school.

Somehow, he'd managed to keep it together, enough to look after his mum. Enough to finish with grades and friendships intact. Enough to finally put an end to it.

But if going back helped him figure out why Harper sometimes looked at him like he had horns, he'd do it.

"Tell me."

"Why? So you can throw it in my face? Been there. Never want to go there again."

Battling a chaotic mix of concern and frustration, Cormac crossed his arms, the cotton stretching tight over muscle and bone. His voice was quiet but the intent clear as he said, "Are you just going to leave that there like a little time bomb? Or do you plan to tell me what that's supposed to mean?"

She lifted her chin. "It's nothing."

"It sounded pretty specific. Did I cut in front of you in the lunch line? Did you ask me to a school dance and I was already taken?"

She'd have been such a spitfire back then. Full of hope and promise and snark. Why hadn't he seen her? Noticed her? Especially if she'd had a crush on him. The very thought of which was messing with his head, big time.

He'd been a swimming star, part of the "in" group, and he'd had all his features in the right place. He'd seen enough John Hughes movies to understand those ingredients all but ensured that girls would giggle behind their hands as he and his mates walked past.

And yet knowing that one girl in particular had harboured feelings for him made him feel as if the fabric of his life was being stretched out of shape.

"Harper, sweetheart. Just tell me."

For a moment he thought she hadn't heard, or was going to refuse him again, but then her voice came to him, soft but clear.

"It was late in your last year of high school, right before graduation. You must remember the scandal. My family's scandal."

"I promise you I'm not making light, but I remember very little of that time." He swallowed, knowing there was only one way she'd believe him. "My father... That year was his worst."

She glanced his way, her eyes impossible to

read in the semi-darkness. And she said, "Mine too. My dad lost everything—every cent we had and then some—in a shady real-estate deal."

Harper's father—*Lola's father*—had gone *broke*? No. Surely he'd have remembered that. Or at least learnt about it since. If the Chadwicks knew they'd have said something, for they'd never held back business talk in front of him. They'd always treated him as if his opinion mattered. Taught him that, armed with knowledge, he could make a difference.

"It was all over the news," Harper said. "All over the school. My father lost millions, not only his own money but also that of a number of local mum and dad investors, too."

When her gaze swept to his, moonlight glowing at the edges of the dark depths, he found himself holding his breath.

"It was awful," she said. "Everyone knew. It was too much for Dad to bear, and he left."

"Left."

She nodded.

"I don't understand. You were what, sixteen? Lola younger again. Your mother wasn't around and he *walked out*."

"And never came back."

Her eyes remained focussed on his. Watchful. As if trying to decipher how much he was hiding from her about not remembering. As if he wasn't the only one who struggled with trust.

"Wow, you *really* don't remember, do you?"

He shook his head. And once again said, "Tell me."

"News spread fast, as it does in this place, and the scavengers arrived the next day to clear us out. I don't even know who they were. I thought it was the bank, but looking back it couldn't have been. Loan sharks, perhaps. Worse. We were probably lucky we weren't cleared out with the stuff.

"I only managed to fill a couple of backpacks as they took everything. Our furniture. My stereo. Lola's soft toys. Even the family photographs. I'm sure they had lost money in Dad's deal, as it was personal.

"Anyway, I had to find Lola and myself somewhere to sleep. I negotiated with the market on Haynes Street. I already worked there after school and weekends only from that time on I'd do so for use of the vacant space above the store and a grocery allowance.

"I didn't realise till we were getting ready for school on the Monday that I'd only packed clothes for Lola. The only clothes were the ones on my back-old jeans and an ancient Bowie T-shirt of my mum's. I washed them every night. Wore them to school still damp if necessary. One day I was sent home—half-day suspension, no less—because my shirt was too short. Only because it had shrunk from so many washes."

"The speech," he said, under his breath. "The one about sexist uniform policies."

She blinked at him, a ghost of a smile flickering across her lush mouth.

"The shop owner downstairs heard and gave me a bag of hand-me-downs. And they started paying me my wage again as well. Thank goodness, because it meant Lola had money for excursions and birthday parties and dental check-ups. All the while I had to avoid any questions about guardianship."

Cormac ran a hand through his mussed-up hair. He'd thought he'd kept his family turmoil under wraps, but where he'd had his friends to protect him, she'd gone through it on her own.

No wonder she was still so overly concerned about Lola's welfare—she'd been raising her since she was a kid herself.

He had questions. But he kept them to himself. She needed to get this out. He waited, and he listened, all the while his gut roiling with anger at her father, and at his town that had made a sixteen-year-old girl negotiate to put a roof over her head.

All the while dreading the part he'd played in the story she told.

She held her arms around herself, shaking so hard her teeth rattled.

"You're trembling," he said, sliding off the car to be next to her.

"I'm fine."

"Let me get the jacket." He made to move and Harper's hand reached out and grabbed his wrist.

"Stay."

He stayed. He also took her hand in his and held it between his own, rubbing it and blowing hot air over her chilled skin.

She watched him as she said, "It was a few weeks after. I saw you at that table under the oak tree—"

"Behind the science block."

"Right. You were sitting on the table, feet on the bench, legs jiggling with pent-up energy. You were wearing your Jurassic Fart T-shirt."

Cormac grimaced. He didn't remember much from that year, but he remembered that shirt. *If she remembers that much detail, this is going to be bad.*

"You were wild-eyed. Unfocussed. You looked like you wanted to climb out of your skin. I'd never seen you like that before. You looked… You looked how I felt. Your friends, on the other hand, all sat on the grass nearby, joking, lying all over one another, not a care in the world. The fact that none of them saw you, saw how tragic you looked, well, it made me angry. So…"

She glanced at him then, chin ducked, eyes blinking. First time he'd ever seen her look shy. He moved in a little closer, ran his hand down her forearm and back up again, thawing her out an inch at a time.

"So I went up to you. And I asked if you were okay. You looked through me like I was some kind of apparition. Then one of the others, a boy— not Gray, Josh—jumped up and loped over. Said something like, *'What's up, Addison? Begging for the whales? The spotted owl? Or lunch money?'*"

"What the—?"

Harper waved it off. As if in the grand scheme of things Josh the douche had barely left a mark. "A place like Blue Moon Bay High you can't get away with wearing the same clothes every day before it becomes a point of conversation. Then he turned to you and said, *'What do you reckon, Wharton? Should we give her what she wants?'*"

Cormac's jaw hardened. "Please tell me I told him where to go."

"Not exactly." Harper's next breath in was short, sharp; as if the sensation burned. "You looked me dead in the eye and said, *'She's nobody. She's not getting anything from me.'*"

Cormac stilled; his entire body felt like ice, only now it was her warm hand in his keeping him tethered.

He slid his hand up her arm, and gently tugged her closer. Right into the curve of his body. He waited for her to twist away. Would let her go in an instant if she did. But after a moment she gave in, settling into his side, her head tucked under his chin.

"I said that?" he asked, his words muffled by her hair.

She nodded against his shoulder. "Word for word."

Cormac closed his eyes and tried to picture the time, the day, the way it might have unfolded. It wasn't hard. She had recounted it in excruciating detail.

"Josh wasn't exactly a friend of mine," he said, his voice rough. "He was a drifter in the group. He could be a git even at the best of times. And for some reason he always treated me more like competition than a friend."

"Tara," Harper said, her voice a husky whisper. *Of course.*

Cormac breathed in the scent of her hair, letting his mouth rest against her crown a moment before he said, "If Josh thought you meant something to me, he'd have made your life hell."

Harper's face tilted to his, and she stared hard into his eyes. He wondered what he saw. What she made of him. Then and now. It floored him how much it mattered.

"But I *didn't* mean anything to you," she said. "And yet... Are you telling me you were trying to *protect* me? Even so?"

"If Josh was about to cause trouble, with anyone, taking the fun out of it was always a good way to deflate it."

Harper's deep eyes gleamed in the low light.

Her arm rubbed against his chest as she breathed in and out. Her skin, no longer ice-cold, burned him everywhere they touched.

And then she laughed, the sound closer to a sob. Laughed and laughed and laughed. Before, with a groan, she leant forward, her face falling into her hands.

Cormac's hand slid to her back. To the satiny touch of her dress. Beneath the thin fabric he felt the delicate curve of her spine. Felt her every breath.

He opened his mouth to ask if she was okay, then closed it. She wasn't okay. It had been clear from the moment she arrived. Only now he knew why.

She pulled herself upright. Cormac's hand slid to her hip. He took the chance to pull her closer. She let him. Melting against him as if she no longer had the strength to hold herself up.

Eventually she said, "My life took a turn that day. I hardened up, my focus becoming a pinpoint of determination. I'd show my mum, I'd show my dad, I'd show you that I wasn't someone to walk away from, to dismiss. I wasn't nobody."

Cormac had been made to feel worthless in his life. Told by his father on a near daily basis in the end, how disappointing he was, how insignificant, he'd come all too close to letting himself give in and believe it.

The good people in his life—the Grays, the

Adeles, the core gang—had been the reason he'd been able to break free.

From what he'd gathered she'd not had that. She'd been too busy trying to hold her family together to make friends like his. To think he'd been the one who made her feel small when she'd had no people, no support—he felt as if claws were tearing at his insides.

"Harper."

"What?"

"Look at me."

She heaved in a deep breath and looked up into his eyes, fierce and utterly wondrous. And something ferocious and unstoppable stampeded through his chest.

Gray thought her a Hitchcockian ice queen, but Cormac knew better. Harper Addison was pure fire. And that fire of hers had lit something within him, stoking the embers of the slow burn of a life he'd thought was enough. The life he'd thought was exactly as he wanted it to be.

She'd wrapped an invisible fist around something deep and primal inside of him and yanked him out of complacency without even trying.

Cormac's hand travelled slowly up her back, catching on the ribbon at her neck before sliding back down. He saw smoke drift into her eyes—eyes that were wide open, exposed—and felt change in the very vibrations in the air.

Her crush was not merely a thing of the past.

His crush, on the other hand, was brand new. And all the more mercurial, unwieldy and unsettling for it.

He wanted to kiss her, more than he remembered wanting anything in his entire life. It took every gentlemanly bone in his body not to take advantage.

For there were more things to say.

"While it doesn't excuse the way I made you feel that day, will you allow me to give you some context?"

She nodded. "Okay."

"It was right around the time you described that I finally convinced Mum to leave my father. I'd spent a rough few months working her up to it, securing a room in a domestic-violence shelter. I took the day off school to drive her there—three hours away to a place he'd never find her. At eighteen, six-feet-two and male, I wasn't allowed to stay with her which was hard. But she convinced me I had to go home, to graduate with my friends. And I wanted to see the look in his eyes when he realised she was gone."

Harper asked, "What happened?"

"It went as was to be expected." He lifted a hand to his forehead.

Her fingers followed, tracing the pale line that slashed through his eyebrow. "Your *father* did that?"

And more. Before then, before he'd come home

to find his wife gone he'd been lucid enough to make sure the scars would be well hidden. "Broken bottle. He was aiming for my throat. Swing and a near miss."

"Except for the black eye."

"Hmm?"

"I remember now. You had a black eye. That day. It was so unlike you it was why I'd found the courage to go up to you in the first place. I was a sucker for a lost cause."

He tried again to imagine her. A girl with a heart big enough to put aside the horrors she was dealing with to check on him. While his friends— too distracted by all the end-of-high-school excitement—hadn't noticed a thing.

"I slept in the local park after the bottle incident," he said, his voice sounding far away to his own ears. "The noises you hear outside your window as a kid are nothing compared to being up close and personal."

Harper said nothing. She simply turned in his arms until she leaned flush against him. One hand sliding over his shoulder, the other gathering his hand and holding it to her chest.

"The next day Gray took one look at me and dragged me back to his folks' place. They offered me a room in the house, but I couldn't take it. I'd been trapped for so long, I feared I'd wake in the middle of the night and smash a window to get

out. So they gave me the pool house—a room of windows and light—for as long as I wanted it."

"The pool house," she murmured. "It always sounded so decadent."

Her voice reverberated through his chest.

"It was the Chadwicks' pool house. Of course it was decadent."

Her eyes lifted to his. Maybe it was the moonlight playing tricks, but there was no wall up now. Only so much tenderness his breath stuck in his throat.

Her voice was husky as she said, "No wonder you're so enamoured of them."

"The Chadwicks are the reason I'm here today. All three of them. They are the reason I came back here, to the edge of the world. Without them…who knows what might have become of me?"

Harper's dark eyes flickered between his. "For so long I've dreamed of telling you off for how you treated me. Mostly because you left before I had the chance."

Her voice cracked on the words "you left". And no wonder. Her mother had left. Her father had left. How many times could that happen to a person and they still forged on? Only she'd more than forged on, she'd flourished. She'd shown them all.

"And now?" he asked.

"I've always believed my life took a turn that day. A turn on a misunderstanding, as it turns out. Does that make my entire life a sham?"

He reached up and unhooked a strand of golden hair from her eyelashes. "It makes you human."

"Who knew?" Harper said, her voice husky, her eyes darkening. There was a softness about her he'd not seen before. A yielding.

And Cormac knew in that moment that he was in deep, deep trouble.

He'd told Gray nothing would happen between him and Harper because he'd believed it wasn't worth the trouble.

Now he knew nothing could happen between them because he might never get over it.

For Cormac was a man who held on to those who'd marked him in some way, taking on the cuts and bruises along with the laughter and light. For they had all helped forge the man he'd become.

He knew if he let Harper in, she'd carve him to pieces. And when she left she'd take whatever pieces of him she wanted.

"Thank-you for telling me," he said, his voice rough.

She nodded.

"It's late. We should get word to Lola and Gray, let them know we're okay. Then I should get you home."

At mention of Lola, he felt the shift. All but saw the wall slide back down between them.

"Right," she said, gently pressing away. "Let's do that."

Once completely free of him, she ran a hand

over her dress, fixed her hair, until everything was perfectly in place once more. Then strode around the car and hopped inside.

His phone buzzed. A quick check of the message had him frowning. "Dammit."

"What's wrong?"

He leapt into the driver's seat without opening the door, and had the engine ticking over in a second. He looked over his shoulder as he made a quick turn and took off back down the dirt path.

"Mind if we make a quick stop? The alarm has gone off at my place."

"Your place?"

"My house. My home."

"So you really did move out of the pool house, then? I thought you were kidding."

The snark was back. Though it was half-hearted. As if she couldn't quite tap into it any more. As if things had shifted too far towards something intimate. Something real.

Cormac carefully navigated the rutted path as they made their way back towards the coastal road. And felt a sense of inevitability fall over him at the thought of taking her home.

CHAPTER NINE

HARPER FELT AS if her life had been shaken like a snow globe. As the flakes settled, everything looked different.

Her father had always been fickle. When he fell short it was a disappointment, but not a shock.

Cormac had been her constant. A shining light in her topsy-turvy world. So much so she'd built him into something unrealistic. A person without fault. Without pain. Without troubles of his own.

And the first time he'd faltered she'd cracked.

Only Cormac *hadn't* faltered; he'd been trying to protect her even as he'd lived inside his own pain.

What if she'd known? What if she'd taken another step towards him, rather than walking away? Might something have been forged from that moment, rather than being broken?

So deep inside her own head was she, Harper paid no attention to where Cormac was taking her until the car rumbled to a stop.

"Back in a sec," he said as he hopped out of the car to meet a security guard before the men headed inside.

Harper slid numbly out of the car, gaze dancing

over a gorgeous big liquid amber tree—tyre swing and all—in the pristine front yard. Front porch. Gabled roof. Big, neat suburban home.

Harper was halfway up the path when the security guy came back out. He smiled, tipped his hat and jogged back to his little white hatchback, but not before slowing to have a quick look over Cormac's far cooler wheels.

"Hello?" Harper called as she stepped through the open front door.

"Back here."

Harper followed Cormac's disembodied voice up a wide hall boasting pale wood floors, and warm, creamy walls. She spied couches and rugs in living spaces, a tidy open-plan office. Fireplaces everywhere. And in a media room a wall of movie posters—art deco takes on *Vertigo*, *Rear Window*, *Dial M for Murder*.

The house was both elegant and comfortable. But what stood out most of all was the sheer scope for just one man.

It was not a house for a bachelor. It was a house for a family.

Still unbalanced from earlier, and now even more so at having to place this piece into the Cormac puzzle, Harper found the man in question turning lights on in a large chef's kitchen.

"No burglar?" she asked.

He glanced up, his expression unreadable as he watched her walk towards him. "Just a dog who can open fridge doors." Then he held up a carton of orange juice, the drink dripping from a hole in the corner.

Harper saw movement out of the corner of her eye and turned to find Novak lying on a big, soft doggy bed, looking guilty.

"Who's a clever girl?" Harper said on a laugh.

Taking it as an invitation, Novak slunk up to her, leaned gently against her leg and looked up at her for a pat. As Harper looked down into the dog's liquid eyes, she felt herself fall in love, just a little bit.

When she looked up to find Cormac standing still as a statue, watching her, brow furrowed, eyes dark and consuming, she didn't steel her heart against the sight of him nearly quickly enough.

"So this little piece of suburbia is really yours?" she asked.

"I bought it for my mum, actually."

"She lives here with you?"

"No," he said with a wry smile. "She's only been here once. The day I planned to surprise her with the place. Before I had the chance, she told me she was getting remarried. To a guy I'd never even met. She was standing about where you are, right now."

Harper took a step sideways. "Yet you kept it."

"I'd bought it for her." The words were simple, the sentiment anything but.

Cormac Wharton was no cardboard cut-out to

drool over. He was far deeper than she'd given him credit for. He was a man who put great stead in his place in the world. His purpose. His tribe.

His family.

No wonder he'd found the Chadwicks so compelling—with their big smiles and warm hugs.

After the craziness of their childhood, no wonder Lola had too.

"Did you tell her?" Harper asked, very much needing a distraction. "Did you end up telling your mum what you'd done?"

Cormac shook his head. "Didn't seem right to burden her. Not when the point had been to gift her her freedom. I wonder though if she'd have taken it anyway. If one of the reasons she's been away so long is that she looks at me and sees him."

Him. His father.

Harper's father had been imperfect. But he'd tried to make their lives fun and bright and joyful. Tried to love them enough that the rest didn't matter.

While, from what Harper could glean, Cormac's father had hit his mother until Cormac was big enough to take the brunt. And he'd taken it, refusing to leave until he could convince his mother to do the same.

Yet under the kitchen down lights Cormac couldn't hide the shadows in his eyes. The regret, the hurt, the sliver of uncertainty that maybe his mother was right.

"You want to know why I had such a crush on you in high school?" The words spilled out of her before she even felt them forming. "It wasn't because you were cute, though you were that. It wasn't because you were popular, though I never heard anyone say a bad word about you. It was because you were kind. To everyone from the groundskeeper to the principal."

Always quick with a joke, with a smile and a way to lighten the mood, Cormac didn't budge. So Harper did, taking a step his way.

"At my house we'd have chocolate cake for dinner one night, nothing at all the next. The place could have been filled with balloons and streamers and glitter all over the floor when Dad was in a good mood, or deathly quiet if he was having one of his 'dark days'. Never knowing what I'd come home to, high school for me was a torrent of quiet tension. Except when I saw you."

A muscle ticked at the edge of his jaw. And Harper kept walking towards the kitchen.

"You have a way of making people feel calm, Cormac. Feel safe. Feel as if it's all going to be okay. There is no possible way your mother looks at you and sees anyone but you."

She turned the corner of the bench on her last word, only to stop at the sight of the devastation on the kitchen floor. "Wow, that dog of yours doesn't do things by halves."

Cormac blinked at her. Then laughed. Then ran

a hand over his face. Then let out a little growl. Sexiest five seconds of Harper's entire life.

He watched her then, across the kitchen, for a heartbeat. And another. Before he breathed out hard. And asked, "Are you thirsty? Hungry?"

Harper was both. At least, she told herself that was the gnawing feeling in her belly. That big, empty hole that hadn't been there a week ago.

"I could eat."

"Then go," he said, angling his chin towards the front room. "Sit. Put on a movie. I'll finish cleaning then I'll whip something up." He didn't reiterate his plans to drop her home after.

Then again, neither did she.

"You cook? More than your famous ham sandwiches you once tried to tempt me with?"

"I reheat," he said, poking a thumb at his freezer. "I'm pretty damn good at it too."

With a smile and a nod she turned on her heel and moseyed back to the front room, where she turned on the TV and scrolled through his movie library till she found the one she was looking for.

She kicked off her shoes and tucked herself up on the couch, smiling as Cary Grant and Grace Kelly's names appeared on the screen.

Cormac picked up the opening strains of *To Catch a Thief* within the first couple of bars. He smiled. The woman had taste.

His subconscious spoke up. *Clearly. She had a crush on you, after all.*

His foot moved and slipped slightly in a blob of cream. Crush magnet or not, he still had to clean his own damn kitchen.

His kitchen; not his mother's. It was time he got used to that fact.

To the fact his mother had done exactly what he'd always hoped she could. To stand up for what she wanted. To turn her back on the past. To find a way to be happy.

He'd just never imagined it would mean turning her back on him.

A woman screamed in the front room—a woman in the movie, not Harper.

Harper. She'd been left by her mother, *and* her father. Both before she was even an adult herself. And, rather than giving in, she had chosen to fight for the right to forge a life for herself. A highly successful life, by the sound of it. All the while making sure Lola had the chance to do the same.

When had Cormac last fought for anything? Fair pay, yes. Workers' rights, sure. But something real to him? Something personal?

He'd spent years priding himself on his contentment. But contentment was easy. It didn't ask too much of a person. While Harper… Harper expected more.

Harper was real. As real a person as he'd ever

known. And once upon a time she'd thought the same about him.

How does she see you now? How does she feel about you now? What does it matter? She'll be gone in a few days, and you'll be here. Always here...

His subconscious sure was chatty tonight.

Cormac motioned to Novak, who hustled over, panting happily, ears flicking up and down, between guilty and delighted. He reached out and gave her ear a quick rub. She blinked, one eye at a time.

"Have at it," Cormac said.

Novak did as instructed, delicately lapping up the edible bits while Cormac cleaned up the rest. Then he let her out into the big back yard to do her nightly security check.

The soundtrack of the movie grew louder as he neared the front room. And there he found Harper, curled up on his couch, fast asleep.

Her cheek rested against the back of the couch, her hair tumbled over one cheek, her bare feet curled around one another.

He laughed under his breath at the way she white-knuckled the cushion cuddled to her chest. Tightly wound, even in sleep. As if the world might scatter into a zillion tiny little particles if she wasn't there to hold it all together.

He found the remote and tuned the sound to low, then he slowly sat on the empty end of the couch nearest her head, draping his arm along the back of the couch.

The movement unsettling her, she woke. Eyes flickering open. Whole body stretching. Elegant, graceful, and beguiling.

When her eyes snagged on his they stuck. For a second or two, she was completely open, her eyes drinking him in, her face softening into a smile so true it made his heart twist.

"Hi," she said, her voice husky and light.

"Hi."

"What happened?"

"You fell asleep."

"I did?"

"Mmm-hmm. I'd chastise you for daring to do so during one of the best movies ever made but I have the feeling you needed the rest."

She shifted, pulling herself upright until her face was level with his. "How long was I out?"

"Not long."

"I was dreaming."

"About?"

Her gaze roved over his face before landing back on his eyes. "I'd rather not say."

She didn't have to. It was written all over her face.

"Can I ask you something?" she said, looking around the room. "I know why you stayed, but what brought you back in the first place? Was it a girl?"

"No, Harper. I didn't come back for a girl."

"So, you're not living here, alone in this big family house, because you're pining for the one that got away?"

"And who do you imagine that might be?" he asked, voice soft, low.

Her lips snapped together, as if only just realising how much she was revealing. "I'm just trying to build a profile here."

"A profile?"

"I meant picture."

"No, you didn't."

"Fine. It's what I do. I research everyone in the room so I know what I'm up against."

"And you're planning to go up against me?"

The double entendre was not subtle. The waggling eyebrows made it even less so.

Harper managed a deadpan stare. "Do you wish things had worked out differently with Tara?"

"Did I not mention the four sons under five?"

He saw the smile hit her eyes first before it tugged at one corner of her lush mouth. Cormac's gaze dropped to the tug. Stayed as Harper said, "Even so."

He tugged on a curl, as if using it to lever himself forward. Her nostrils flared, but she didn't back away.

"Harper, are you asking if I still have feelings for my high-school girlfriend?"

"I'm merely making conversation."

"I'd not have pegged you for a fan of small talk."

"Needs must."

A slow smile spread across his face. "Interesting saying, that one. *Needs must.* Why is that that you *need* to know if I'm seeing anyone? Why *must* you know if there's anyone I'm longing for? Only one reason I can think of."

She licked her lips before asking, "And what's that?"

"Because that crush of yours is still well and truly alive."

She breathed out hard, her molten gaze dropping to his mouth.

He waited for her to fight him, for she was nothing if not a fighter. He waited for her to deny every word, for denial was a fair part of her repertoire. But she didn't. She sat there on his couch, hugging his cushion. And for the life of him he couldn't remember his own name, much less the name of any other girl he'd ever met.

"Here's something for you to mull over," he said, sliding his hand deeper into her satiny hair. "I have a crush on you, too."

Her lips opened on a sigh.

"And if you don't want me to kiss you till neither one of us remembers how we got here, now's the time to tell me."

Out of the corner of his eye he saw her grip soften on the cushion, before she flung it across the room.

Then she reached up, slid a hand around the

back of his neck, and she kissed him. Open-mouthed. Soft, sensual, hot as Hades.

With a growl he took her in his arms, shifting until she lay beneath him on the couch. His thigh between hers. Her leg wrapping around his, trapping him. Claiming him.

Then, like teenagers, they couldn't get enough of one another. All harsh breath and clashing tongues. Roving hands and raging lust.

Needing to calm things, to centre himself, before he lost himself entirely, Cormac ran a settling hand over her shoulder, down her bare arm, till his hand reached her thigh, her bare thigh. Her satiny dress had ridden up until his thumb brushed the slightest, most delicate hint of lace before it gave way to the curve of backside.

Afraid it might end him, then and there, he kept his hand moving until he found her hand, took it, lifting it to his lips. Placing a kiss on the tip of each finger, before resting his lips on her palm.

She watched him, chest rising and falling, eyes bright. Overly bright, as if she might be about to…

With a shake of her head she broke eye contact, then pushed him to sitting. There she wasted no time before undoing the buttons on his shirt.

"Harper," he said, lifting a hand to cup her cheek.

"Shut up, Cormac," she said, shaking his hand away. "Anyone ever told you you talk too much?"

Cormac coughed out a laugh, the sound barely

making it past the tightness in his chest. "Not a single living soul."

When her eyes found his they were full of fire. Desire. And something else. Something deep and raw and old as the cliffs keeping Blue Moon Bay from tumbling into the raging ocean below.

This woman, he thought as he somehow managed to stop himself from tearing the shirt from his back. To let her do the work. Understanding on a cellular level that a semblance of control was necessary to her. Even while handing it over was unnerving to him.

She slid his shirt down his arms, her thumbs scraping against bare skin as she took her time. Eyes roving hungrily over his chest. His bare stomach. The aching bulge in his jeans. Her hands stopping when they reached his wrists. Trapping him with his shirt so that he couldn't touch her. Like Jimmy Stewart, stuck in his wheelchair, while the most beautiful woman in the world shadowed over him.

"Harper," he murmured. "You are every fantasy I ever had, all rolled into one."

Only this was real life. The woman before him all too real. No ice in her eyes, no wall between them, only heat, and desire, for him.

He leaned in, holding her eyes with his, before he kissed her softly. Gently. Tenderly. Meaningfully.

Waiting until she began to sigh, and moan, and

melt, before carefully pulling a hand free so that he could touch her, run his fingers down her neck, undoing the ribbon at the back of her dress, until the silken slip of nothing pooled at her waist.

Their eyes caught. Neither of them breathed. As if hovering on the brink of something. This their final chance to pull back. To slink back to the safety of their respective corners.

Then Harper lifted her hand to Cormac's cheek, her thumb brushing over his bottom lip before she followed up with a kiss. A caress. An admission.

Then she lay back. A vision of loveliness. Of surrender.

To this. To them.

When Cormac woke it was to a quiet house. The TV was turned off. Novak snored softly on the rug. He didn't need to call out, to search the house, to know that Harper was long gone.

With a groan he unpeeled his long body from the couch, replacing the cushions that had fallen to the floor, before sitting and resting his face in his hands.

How had she managed that? Uber? The town-car guy from Melbourne who'd been so clearly smitten with her? She might well have walked, for all he knew. If she'd wanted to get out that bad, she'd have found a way.

A thought came to him and he was on his feet, padding barefoot to the garage, only breathing out upon finding his beautiful blue Sunbeam slumbering safely there still.

Closing the door, he looked about his big house. He only lived in three or four of the rooms; the rest had never been touched except by a cleaner once every couple of weeks.

But now it seemed cavernous. Empty. A clock ticking somewhere upstairs marking the long seconds as he tried to measure how he felt.

All too quickly landing on restless. Off kilter. Discontent.

Cormac swore beneath his breath as he picked up the clothes strewn about the lounge before jogging up the stairs to his bedroom. Heading straight into the *en suite,* he dumped his clothes in the hamper, before turning the spray to full hot.

She needn't have stayed over if that had been her concern. Hell, he'd have been happy to take her wherever she wanted to go. Well, not happy, but resigned.

At the very least she could have woken him. Said goodbye.

But even as he thought it he knew it wasn't her way.

She might have been a revelation in the quiet dark of night, offering him a rare glimpse at the tender heart of her.

But in the bright light of day she was a runner. It was in her blood, after all.

CHAPTER TEN

LOLA TURNED HER face to the sharp summer sunshine. "Can you believe this weather? I mean, tell me, have you seen skies like this anywhere else in the world?"

Harper grimaced as she tugged the spike of her left heel out of the lush lawn leading out to the Chadwicks' extensive rear gardens. "Hmm?"

Lola dropped her hands to her yoga-pants-clad hips. "You're the one who said you wanted to get some fresh air—now you're acting like you're allergic."

"I know. And I do." She did want fresh air. Or at least some space to talk to Lola without wondering if someone was about to walk in the room. The nature she could take or leave.

Harper winced as something landed on her shoulder.

Lola leaned forward to flick away the small leaf, then tucked a hand in the crook of her arm. "Come on, Harps, let's just walk and you can tell me why we're out here when you're ready."

Lola yabbered away about the lemon icing she'd chosen for the wedding cake, and the gorgeous local bubbly they'd chosen over imported champagne.

Harper tried to concentrate, but she couldn't stop her mind from wandering to Cormac. His couch. To making love to Cormac on his couch.

For that was what it had felt like. Not sex. Not a one-night stand or an itch that had needed scratching. But sweet and gentle. Tender and thorough. It had also been seductive, and hot, and gravely intimate. Consuming. Till every cell in her body, every ounce of her soul had come together to ride the wave of heat and feeling and emotion.

When she'd woken to find herself curled up in Cormac's arms, she'd felt as if she'd been jolted with an open electrical wire and when she'd come back to earth all of her cells had settled in the wrong place. A place that craved his protection, his warmth, his intimacy.

"Harper, what's got into you?" Lola asked. "First you disappear on me last night without a word. Then you don't come home. I knew you were with Cormac and he's the last person in the world who'd let anything bad happen to you, but what the heck is going on?"

"Nothing. I'm fine. Just worried about you."

Way to deflect.

Though somehow it worked. "Harps, I'm on the countdown to marrying the man of my dreams. What could I possibly have to worry about?"

As openings went, it was too good to pass up.

Harper looked back at the house, looming ominous and regal on its agrestic bluff, and she felt a flicker of guilt. Her mind went to Cormac and his stories of how the Chadwicks had saved his life. To Gray, and the way he looked at Lola, with such tenderness and indulgence.

But then she saw herself as a sixteen-year-old girl, sitting on the floor of the downstairs bathroom, trying to stop her father crying, while he shouted the name Weston Chadwick, crying into his hands as he blamed the man for ruining his life.

She would never forgive herself if she had brought Lola this far only to let her down at such a critical moment.

"Lola, honey, can we talk seriously for a moment?"

Lola's eyes flickered before she said, "I know what this is about."

"You do?"

"It's Cormac. It's not just a crush for you. You're smitten with the guy."

"That's not it at all—"

"But it's true."

"Fine. Yes. I guess. But—"

"You guys totally got it on last night, didn't you?"

Harper gawped, no longer in control of her faculties.

"Ha! I knew it!" Lola snapped her fingers. "I

was totally sure you'd deny it. When I told Gray I reckoned the two of you had left the party to find somewhere a little more private he was all, *'Nah, they can barely look at one another without biting each other's heads off.'* While I said, *'He looks at her like a lion looks at a baby gazelle—like he wants to swallow her whole.'* And I was right!"

Which was when Harper knew her innate ability to hold her emotions in check had been stuttering for some time. Badly.

Lola grabbed her by both hands, forcing Harper to look her in the eye. "Don't look so stricken! This is the kind of thing we should be able to talk about. Not only your work, and my work, and if I have enough money, and if I'm eating my vegetables. Sisters should dance together, and cry together, and talk about boys. And you need to let me support you as much as you've supported me."

Harper sniffed, gaze flickering between her little sister's eyes. "When did you suddenly become a grown-up?"

Lola shrugged. "Oh, a little while back now."

She didn't say it happened while Harper was on the other side of the world, but the truth of it hovered between them all the same.

Till Lola said, "Enough garden, don't you think? Shall we head back?"

Harper nodded. And on the amble back to the house they talked about work, and they talked about Gray. But they also talked about some of

the fun times they'd had as kids, and some of the
hard times too, the subjects shifting and changing
with the dappled sunshine lighting the path ahead.

Harper realised she hadn't managed to tell Lola
the truth about the Chadwicks. About their part
in her dad's downfall.

She'd find another moment. Soon.

Right now she just wanted to relish the newness
of this feeling. Of this different version of sister-
hood. For the relationship she'd been so fearful of
losing might not be lost. It would simply change.
For the better.

"So how was he?" Lola asked as they neared
the back steps leading up into the house.

Harper didn't need to ask who. A beat went by
before she said, "Transcendental."

"Lucky girl."

"Tell me about it."

"Now go rest. We have the pool party this afternoon. And a fun kids-only evening planned
for tonight."

"Will do." A morning off from the wedding
fun, from Cormac, was a huge relief. For Harper
needed some time. Space. To sort out her head
without him there, messing with her algorithms.
"Now, how tight is your wedding dress?"

"Tight enough."

"Pity. I ordered a pair of punnets of macadamia
ice cream to be delivered here from Ice-Ice Baby

for just a moment such as this. I guess I can eat yours too. Take one for the team."

"Harps, there is no dress in the world tight enough to stop me eating Ice-Ice Baby's macadamia ice cream."

Arm in arm, they jogged up the back stairs of the palatial home and made a left towards the kitchens.

By that afternoon the Chadwicks' back yard had been turned out in a French Riviera meets Beach Blanket Bingo theme for Lola and Gray's pre-wedding pool party.

Rows of jauntily angled striped umbrellas threw patches of shade over the bright green grass. While waiters all in white delivered trays of cocktails and nibbles to the guests clad in everything from Alain Delon open-necked shirts to Sandra Dee pedal-pushers.

"Just a few hundred of your closest friends?" Harper asked.

"Business associates, mostly," said Lola, waving madly as she spotted Gray weaving his way through the crowd, looking dapper in tight board shorts and yellow shirt to match Lola's yellow mini-dress, passing out cigars to anyone who'd take one. "Local community members. The Chadwicks' reach is vast. We wanted the wedding to be intimate. So, this is the compromise."

"Does it worry you that the wedding can't possibly compare to all the pre-wedding parties?"

Lola laughed as she jogged down the stairs, turning to say, "Not a single bit. Now, come on! Let's party!" before she leapt into Gray's arms.

He caught her, twirling her around. Those nearby clapped and laughed. While Lola smiled up at her man as if she was the happiest person on earth.

Seeing Lola happy had been her life's mission for as long as she could remember, and yet Harper found herself having to look away as a strange pain bit behind her ribs. Harper smoothed her hands over her floaty, one-shouldered white dress, before taking the plunge and joining the party.

Dee-Dee Chadwick caught her eye, giving her a big smile and a wave. Weston Chadwick was surrounded with men in linen suits, all laughing at some joke he'd made. When her stomach clenched at the sight of him, Harper looked away.

Gaze dancing over the crowd, Harper searched for a familiar head of preppy chestnut hair. It had been several hours since she'd last seen Cormac. He hadn't called. Then again, neither had she.

Then, weaving her way around the deckchairs by the pool, she found him standing over a BBQ, flipping steaks.

It was so distinctly Australian, so familiar and reassuring, it snagged on something primal inside of her. Then he lifted a beer to his mouth and drank, his lashes batting his cheeks and his throat working against the bubbles. And she had to swallow lest the saliva pooling under her tongue ooze out the corner of her mouth.

As if he'd felt her staring, Cormac turned his head and looked straight at her. And she felt stripped bare. Then steam sizzled between them, obscuring her view of him as if he were a mirage.

With a quick word to one of the others, Cormac handed over the tongs, put down his beer and came to her, every step matching the beat of her heart.

"Harper, you look…stunning."

"Thanks. You too."

And he did. She couldn't have told a soul what he'd been wearing that day but the warmth in his eyes, the intimacy in his smile, made her heart go *kersplat*.

What had she been thinking, sleeping with this man?

Adoring him from afar was one thing. It was safe, harmless. A little heartbreak the worst thing that could come of it.

But, having been with him, having felt his heart beat beneath her hand, having seen the heat in his eyes as he was inside her—she feared for how it would feel to see this end.

With a hand at her elbow he moved her a little further from the barbecue and prying ears. "I wish you'd woken me before you left last night."

"You were out for the count. I thought it best to let you sleep."

"No, you didn't," he murmured, stepping a little closer. Close enough she could see the shadows in his eyes. The sexy stubble shading his jaw. "You turned tail and ran. And there I'd been thinking we'd both had a good time."

"We did. *I* did. I just…" Her words petered out, as she had no excuse apart from pure and unadulterated panic about feeling too much.

"It's okay." He lifted a hand, brushed his knuckles over her cheek.

It sent a sharp tingle sweeping through her body, wild and wanton and needy. She took a step back. Only she'd misjudged, her foot reaching out and finding…nothing.

Her heart leapt into her throat. Her hips shot back, her hands scrambling for something, anything to grab onto. Finding Cormac's shirt.

Instinct had her gripping on tight. His eyes widened. He stepped into her. Her balance gave way and together they tumbled into the pool.

Cool water rushed into her nostrils, into her mouth. Until a pair of strong hands gripped her under the arms and dragged her to the surface.

Harper came up spluttering, her hair all over her face, her hands busy keeping her dress from floating up to her neck. Especially now the entire party had moved to the edge of the pool. Some faces wide with surprise. With embarrassment. Others laughing.

And there, front and centre, Weston Chadwick.

His voice—big and booming—carried across the yard as he said, "In case you haven't met them yet, I give you Harper and Cormac—our maid of honour and best man. And apparently contenders for the family synchronised swimming team. Anyone else want a dip, feel free."

Barely a beat went by before a few men took off shirts, and women slipped dresses over their heads—thankfully revealing swimwear beneath.

Smart move, Harper thought, knowing her bikini was still inside.

Then hands were pressing the swathes of lank wet hair from her face. Cormac's hands. His touch gentle but sure. The pads of his palms deliciously rough. The goosebumps trailing in their wake making her shiver.

Then his hands lingered, smoothing over her skull as if looking for bumps.

When they trailed down the sides of her face, his thumbs smoothing over her temples, his little fingers resting along the edges of her jaw, there was no pretence of examination in the touch. He touched her because he wanted to. He touched her because he could.

She held her breath. Wondered if she might hold it for ever.

"If you ask me if I'm okay," Harper gritted out, "I will scream."

His gaze dropped to her mouth, his nostrils flaring, and she knew he was remembering another way he'd proven himself able to make her scream. Then a smile crinkled the corners of his eyes and he said, "I know you're okay. You'll always be okay. No matter what. It's one of the reasons I can't get enough of you."

With a firm hand, Cormac herded her towards the far edge of the pool, away from the crowd. While Harper was so busy trying to digest his last words, she let him.

He heaved himself out of the pool first. Muscles in his arms bunching, clothes sucked tight to strong legs and a grade-A backside. To think she'd run her hands over all that, again and again, as if committing his shape to memory.

Then he ran a hand over his hair, droplets flying into the sunshine. When he looked back at her, her brain refused to believe he was real.

He pulled his shirt over his head the way men did—two hands behind his neck and tugging forward—before rolling it into a ball and tossing it onto a spare deckchair.

She couldn't *not* stare at his chest, with its spray of dark hair, his washboard stomach, the happy trail that arrowed into his tight shorts. It was right there after all. While every other part of her was soaked through, her mouth went dry.

Then he leaned down and held out a hand.

Harper bit her lip before saying, "I'm not sure I can."

A flicker of humour lit the depths of his eyes. "And why is that?"

"I'm wet."

"So I see."

"This dress is rather…thin. And I'm not wearing any togs." Or a bra, for that matter.

His gaze lowered, that muscle in his cheek clenching as he realised it too.

"Would you prefer I closed my eyes?" Before waiting for an answer he did just that, waggling his hand her way, before squinting one eye open, just a tad.

"It's not you I'm worried about. You've seen it all already."

His eyes popped open. Dark, warm, and full of the knowledge of her.

Knowing it was several hours before sunset, a time when she might exit the pool in semi-darkness, Harper figured her only choice was to suck it up and get the hell out.

No way was she going to let him heave her out of the pool like a seal. She hiked her dress up into a knot at her thigh and waded to the shallows. Water dragging at her, she stepped out as gracefully as possible—meaning not in the least. Tugging her dress down as best she could, she made a beeline for the house.

She felt Cormac fall into line beside her.

"I'm fine," she said; "I don't need an escort."

"Super. Neither do I."

She tried to ignore the titters as they walked through the crowd. But she didn't have enough hands to cover the bits of her the wet white dress revealed.

Out of the corner of her eye she saw Dee-Dee Chadwick rushing over, and Cormac holding out a hand, his head shaking just a little. And just like that, Dee-Dee stopped.

"Can you hold up?" he said.

"I'd really rather not."

"Harper, wait for one second," Cormac said, his frustration with her coming through loud and clear.

She stopped so fast he had to back up.

"What?"

Shaking his head at her, he looked at her as if she was nuts. As if she was stunning, and funny, confounding and nuts.

Then he held out a towel he must have gathered along the way, flicked it out flat and wrapped it around her shoulders. It was soft and warm from the sun.

Holding her by the upper arms, his face mere inches from hers, Cormac said, "I'm going inside with you. We are both getting out of these wet clothes. And then we are going to have a discussion, you and I."

We'll see, she thought. Without a word they made their way up the stairs, turning as one towards her bedroom.

He slowed as Harper headed into the bathroom on her own. When she caught sight of herself in the mirror she let out a squeal.

"What?" he called, rushing to the door.

"I look like a nightmare."

Cormac leant in the doorway. "You look like a water nymph."

She looked at him in the mirror.

"A mess of a nymph, sure. A little insecure. A little out of control. Beautifully fragile."

Cormac couldn't have used a more terrifying word to describe her if he tried.

"Don't you mean brittle?" She'd had that one hurled at her more than once. Enough times she'd wondered if they might be right.

"No, Harper. I don't."

She caught his gaze in the mirror. Raw, honest and scorching hot.

"Don't look at me like that."

"Like what?"

"Like you're waiting for me to take off my wet dress."

"But I am waiting for you to take off your wet dress."

She laughed. Then hiccupped. As if the gods wanted her to know things could still get worse.

Cormac took a step inside the bathroom.

Walked up to her, gently placed his hands on her upper arms as he caught her eye in the mirror. Goosebumps shot up all over her skin and it had nothing to do with the water still dripping down her limbs.

"I thought I made it clear the other day, Harper, that you don't need to pretend to be so perfect. Not with me."

The urge to ask why, why not with him, was so strong it filled her throat so that nothing came out.

He lifted a hand to sweep a wet hank of hair off her neck, his hand resting in the dip at her shoulder as his eyes rose to hers.

She hiccupped again.

Cormac smiled.

And the words spilled free. "I am a mess."

"That you are."

"I don't mean the hair. Or the dress. Or the make-up running down my face."

"I know."

"You do?"

He nodded.

"I came here on a mission," she said, lifting a hand to her heart. Not that she'd tell him what it was. For she'd still not completed it. "But from the moment I stepped out of the car I've felt… disorientated."

Cormac breathed, his hand lifting to tuck around hers, the backs of his knuckles pressed over her heart. He waited, as if weighing up whether or not she could handle what he was about to say.

"Is it wrong for me to say that I'm glad to hear that?"

"Yes, that's wrong!"

Harper hiccupped again and Cormac grinned. A flash of white teeth. Of crinkling eyes. Good lord, the man was hot.

"Why, thank you," he said, surprise lighting his voice. And Harper realised she'd said the last bit out loud.

With a groan she tried to sink her head to her chest, but Cormac caught her chin with a finger and lifted it so she had no choice but to look into his eyes. Then he turned her in his arms so there was no mirror getting in the way.

For a few moments they simply drank one another in.

Then Cormac said, "While I never saw you coming."

Harper swallowed. "What does that mean?"

"It feels like a million years ago that I was sitting on my car, muttering under my breath as I waited and waited and waited for Harper Addison, the bolshie, curly-haired do-gooder in the ripped jeans. I had no idea I was really waiting for you."

She wanted to look away, she needed to look away. For, locked in Cormac's gaze, she had nowhere to hide.

Then Cormac said, "I can't rightly say what is

happening here, with us, because I've never been here before. But I feel as if I see you in a way I've never seen anyone before. That you see me in a way no one has seen me before. From the moment you stepped out of that car, and levelled that blistering hazel gaze my way, I have been under your spell. I can't decide if that's wondrous or disastrous."

"Disastrous," she said on a sigh. "Definitely disastrous."

"Okay, then. Glad we got that sorted."

A single note flickered in the back of her brain—a reason she should push him away. Like flotsam in a post-storm sea, it bobbed on the surface a moment before it sank beneath the calming waves and was gone.

Harper felt the tears fill her eyes a mere moment before they spilled warm and wobbly over her cold cheeks. Who was she? She didn't recognise this emotional being in Cormac's arms. Would she ever know herself again?

"Cormac, I—"

"Harper!" Lola called from just outside the room.

"In here," Cormac said, holding her as if he realised she'd collapse without him.

Lola burst in, her eyes full of concern. "What happened? The girls told me Cormac pushed you into the pool." She glared at Cormac, eyes dark and ferocious. Lola as protector; that was new.

Harper quickly swept fingers under her eyes, as if trying to clean up her mascara. "Not exactly how it went down. Though I'm okay if you don't wish to disillusion them."

In the mirror she saw Cormac slip from the room. Felt the loss of him like a phantom limb.

"So you both fell in the pool."

"Mmm-hmm."

"Who took who with them?"

"I took him."

Lola nodded. "Nice."

"She's wet, remember," Cormac's voice called from the bedroom. "And shivering. If you don't get her out of those wet clothes, I—"

"Hey," Gray's deep voice joined the chorus of rescuers. "Lola has this, right, honey?"

"You bet I do, sweetie! You look after Cormac."

"I'm fine," Cormac called back, laughter tinging his deep voice. "I'll be fine."

Lola shut the door with a decisive click before turning on the bath taps.

For someone who was very much used to taking care of herself it was discombobulating. But nice, she realised, no longer having the wherewithal to fight. Really nice. She ran her thumbs beneath her eyes again before letting Lola look after her for once.

CHAPTER ELEVEN

"OH-OH!" LOLA SING-SONGED. "Watch out for a temper tantrum! My sister is *not* a good loser."

"Not a good poker player, you mean," Cormac murmured as he dealt out the cards to the remaining players.

While Harper, who was an extremely adept poker player—her years of learning to read facial tics and tells standing her in good stead—watched as her chips were swept into a pile by Gray. So open-faced a novice could read him, he'd landed a full house and she'd missed it completely.

Harper barely managed to keep it together as he glared Cormac down. "Seriously?"

"What? Are you insinuating it's my fault?" Cormac asked, hand to heart, glint in his eye.

As if she was about to tell the whole table that she'd been distracted by the man playing footsie under the table. How he'd brushed the edge of his hand against her thigh more than once. That every time she'd caught his gaze it had been hot enough to make her blood sizzle.

"Not at all," she said, her voice cool. "You are a paragon of fair play, Mr Wharton."

The corner of his mouth twitched. "A paragon? You do flatter me so."

She quickly pushed away from the table as her cheeks heated condemningly. "Drink, anyone?"

The others—Lola, Gray, Adele and a few others from the old gang—who'd been too busy focussing on their cards to even notice her byplay with Cormac, muttered a range of orders.

Harper headed past the pool table in the huge upstairs games room to the bar, where the barman—yep, they'd kept on an actual bartender after the pool party—poured out the range of cocktails and spirits and Harper's sparkling water.

She glanced over her shoulder to find Cormac watching her, his gaze on her backside. She slunk a hand to her hip. His gaze shot to hers. After which he shook his head, slowly, tellingly, everything he had done to her, everything he still wanted to do, written all over his face.

She spun back to the bar, struggled to catch her breath. To still the thunderous beating of her heart. Which was near impossible when every time she even glanced at the man her very atoms danced and twirled and near spun off into the ether.

Never track down a teenage crush, she thought; a life lesson that ought to be gifted to every woman upon entering adulthood. Along with other absolutes such as the need for financial independence, a quality skin-care regime and shoes that stunned but also fit like a glove.

Speaking of which, Harper nudged off a high heel, curling her toes against the back of her calf. Then asked for a Manhattan. She needed something strong to get her through the rest of this night. For the happy couple didn't seem in any hurry to get to bed, even though the next day they were supposed to be getting married.

Drink in hand, she turned on one foot as she lifted out the stick, and caught the maraschino cherry between her teeth.

Cormac—who was now sitting back in his chair—watched her openly. Eyes dark, breaths long and slow.

Harper bit down on the cherry, her tongue darting out to catch a stray drip as it burst in her mouth.

"Fold," Cormac said, his voice subterranean. Then he threw down his cards, pushed back his chair and strode over to the bar to join her.

Harper quickly tried to find her other high heel with her bare foot but it was nowhere to be found. Meaning she had to balance on one heel, or crane her neck to look into Cormac's face.

So precarious was her self-control when it came to the man, she reached out to grip the bar, choosing precarious balance over giving up high ground.

"Need a hand?" he asked, motioning to the tray of drinks.

"Sure."

He nodded. But didn't make a move bar grabbing his lemon, lime and bitters and taking a sip, turning to lean a hip against the bar himself, so that his body curved towards hers.

She felt his warmth ease over her, around her, into her. It was like nothing she'd ever felt. As if her skin was too tight to hold in all he made her feel.

The fact that she had no control whatsoever over any of it, that another person was able to make her feel so much without her explicit permission, was unsettling. And—she would only ever admit this to herself—rather wondrous.

"Harper?" He nudged her with a knee, then left it there. Touching her. Connecting them. She could feel his energy racing over her skin.

"Hmm?"

"You ready and raring for tomorrow?"

His words were innocuous enough, but Harper knew what he meant. Was she ready to let her little sister go?

"Raring might be pushing it."

"Come on," he said. "Who doesn't love a wedding?"

Having given up on finding her shoe, she'd plopped her bare foot onto the floor. "You mean that, don't you? You are actually looking forward to it."

"Of course I am. The chance to watch two people declare in front of everyone they know—and a few people they don't—that despite the impediments, despite the overwhelming evidence that it is near impossible to sustain, they choose happiness. They choose eternal love."

Harper searched his face for laughter, and found none. "You, Cormac Wharton, are a romantic."

"Unashamedly."

Harper coughed out a laugh. She swallowed the sound, while inside her head it turned into a sob.

She—a realist, a doubter, and fine, a cynic of the highest order—had fallen under the spell of a *romantic*. An honest one. Who said what he felt and meant what he said.

What must that feel like? To have that kind of freedom? To feel that safe in your place in the world?

Harper's entire life had felt like a game of chicken and refusing to flinch first.

Only with Cormac, she'd flinched. She'd flinched big-time. She'd flinched so hard it had knocked her off her axis. Made her forget who she was, what she stood for. He dragged her focus. Made her stumble. Her heart tumble. Until she found herself falling—

Wait, no, she thought, shaking her head. Not *falling*. She wasn't *falling* for him. She was attracted to the man. Who wouldn't be? She even liked him. A great deal.

But falling for the guy would be nothing short

of self-destructive, a streak she did not inherit from either parent, thank you very much.

Across the room Lola slammed her cards on the table and growled. While Adele threw her winning hand onto the table and leapt out of the chair and did a fine impression of an NFL player, post-touchdown.

"I hate this game!" Lola cried, and it could have been Harper sitting there.

Because they were sisters. Family. The only real family either of them had. The only ones who'd never turned their backs on each other. Who'd loved one another no matter what.

Harper didn't want freedom. Not from her. And yet it was coming at her anyway.

Tomorrow Lola would be married. The cord would be cut. And Harper would be truly adrift.

If Lola was grown-up enough to marry, she was grown-up enough to know the truth.

"Whatever it is you are plotting," Cormac said, "stop."

Harper pretended to ignore him as she took a step forward and motioned to Lola.

"You have that manic look in your eye, the kind that makes you look like you're planning world domination." Cormac wrapped a gentle hand around her arm. "What are you up to, Harper?"

"Nothing that concerns you."

"I doubt that very much." His words came with a growl. A growl that tapped into her very marrow.

"Lola!" Harper called.

"Yeah?"

"Need some air?"

Lola ran her hands over her face and pushed her chair back. "Sure."

Harper led her little sister out the door onto the balcony. They were high enough to see over the gardens to the ocean beyond, but the moon was hidden behind a bank of cloud, meaning they could only hear the crashing of the waves against the cliff below.

Lola lifted her face to the sky and took a deep breath. "Can you believe that tomorrow I will be Mrs Grayson Chadwick?"

"Or he could be Mr Lola Addison?"

Lola shot her a look.

"It's been done."

"I'm sure. But not this time. Not by me. I'm happy to take his name. To fold myself into his family."

Harper sucked in a breath through her teeth.

It must have been loud enough for Lola to hear, as she spun and took Harper by the hand and said, "That came out so wrong. I only meant that they've been like family for so long already. Not taking over from you, but as well as you. It's helped, having them, what with you being so far away. I need to belong. To some place. To someone. I'm not like you."

Holding on for all she was worth, Harper managed to say, "There's something I've been meaning to talk to you about. About Gray."

"Gray?"

"His parents actually. And Dad."

"What do Gray's parents have to do with Dad?"

Here goes, Harper thought, nearly one hundred per cent sure this was the right thing to do. "The deal. Dad's deal. It was their fault."

"What are you talking about? Dad lost money, not them. It was awful, but it was unforeseen."

Harper bit her lip, the words clogging her throat. She'd kept Lola in the dark, keeping the family secrets for so long. To protect her. Meaning it was her fault they'd ended up here. Now she had to do her job and fix it.

"I'm certain Dad made that deal on the advice of Weston Chadwick. And when it all went bust he took no responsibility, leaving Dad out to dry."

Lola reared back as if slapped. "That's so not true."

"Not according to Dad."

"You've…?" Lola swallowed. "You've spoken to him?"

"Not since he left, no."

When Lola had rung to say she was getting married, the first thing Harper did was hire an investigator, on the quiet, to track their dad down. To tell him? To invite him? To show him they were both okay despite him? They'd had no luck. She could only hope he was living off the grid some-where. She could only hope he was happy too.

"Oh."

"But back then—the day he came home broken, torn apart—he said so. Over and over again. That it was the Chadwicks' fault. That Weston Chad-wick was to blame."

"I remember," Lola said, her voice barely a whisper.

"You do?"

"I thought it was a dream, or a made-up vi-sion of some sort. Most of my memories of Dad feel like that. Blurs of memory, or fantasy. I have no clue how much is real. But I remember him crying in the bathroom, you kneeling at his feet, gripping his hands, begging him to tell you every-thing so you could fix it. And him…" Lola swal-lowed. "Dad saying that he wished he'd never met Weston Chadwick."

"But you were so young."

"Not that young. I'm only three years younger than you."

"You were always such a happy kid, Lolly. Even during that whole mess. I hoped it all went over your head."

Lola shrugged.

"You see, then, why you can't marry Gray."

"What the hell?" Gray's voice cut across the open space as Adele, Gray and Cormac spilled out onto the balcony, drinks in hand.

Harper's gaze snagged on Cormac's as he slowly shook his head.

"Lola," Harper said.

But Lola gave her a pained look before going to Gray. Harper reached out to grab her hand, to bring her back, to finish the conversation, but her sister slipped through her fingers.

"It's okay," Lola consoled her fiancé. "You just walked in at the wrong moment."

"When would the right moment have been?"

Lola glanced back at Harper, who said, "Tell him. Tell him what I told you. See if he denies it."

"Denies what?" Gray asked, moving to stand in front of Lola. As if needing to protect her— from Harper!

But Lola held up a hand, staying him. "Don't worry about it. She's so used to having control over my life, it's hard for her to stop."

Was she serious?

"For what it's worth, I never wanted to 'control' your life, Lola. It wasn't my childhood dream to work three jobs to pay for rent, food, clothes. Or to hide from Social Services, who'd never have let me look after a thirteen-year-old when I was still underage myself. I wasn't given a choice. Did I say a word when you dropped out of university, a course that I'd paid for, to become a yoga instructor? When you shaved your head? When you came this close to legally changing your name to Bowie?"

Lola's eyes flashed, as if she had more to say but didn't know where to start.

"No," said Harper. "I didn't. But I can't keep quiet about this. I can't stand by and watch as you marry a Chadwick."

"Hey," Gray growled.

Harper hadn't noticed Cormac edging her way until he took a step in front of her. Protecting her. Gray noticed, eyes narrowing at his friend, who had clearly just taken sides.

It was Harper's turn to hold out a hand, to stay him. These men! Had they no clue at all? This wasn't about them.

"Lola," Harper said, "I will stand by you no matter what choices you make for your life. I just want you to have all the facts. I want you to be sure."

"Listen to yourself, Harps. I can't believe you're playing negotiator with me."

"I'm not *playing* at anything."

"Tell me you're not trying to talk me down from the ledge. Grayson is not my version of leaping off a tall building. He's the man I love. Come on, Gray, it's nearly midnight anyway and if you see me a minute after I'll turn into a pumpkin."

Gray gathered Lola into his arms and they left. Adele and the others who'd been watching on from the sidelines seemed to have melted away.

Leaving Harper. And Cormac. And the cool of the night closing in.

"Harper," he said, his voice deep. And disappointed. That cut like nothing else. "What the hell did you just do?"

"I had to tell her the truth."

"What truth?"

"That your precious Chadwicks are the reason my father lost everything."

Cormac ran a hand through his hair, the spikes popping up in its wake. "Says who?"

"Said my father."

"With what evidence?"

Harper looked down at her feet. Her *foot*. She was still wearing only one shoe. She kicked the other one off and watched it bounce pathetically off the balustrade. "He told me so. The night I found him sitting on his bedroom floor in tears. The night before he disappeared for ever. I'd never seen anyone cry like that. Like every tear was a piece of his soul. He looked terrified. Said he'd screwed up and this time there was no way out. And that everything was Weston's fault."

Cormac moved to stand by her, not close enough to touch, but close enough for her to feel him all the same. He leant his arms over the balustrade, looking out into the dark, moonlit grounds. And he said, "From that you took him to mean that it was on Weston's explicit advice that your father made that investment. And after it went bust Weston took no responsibility for his part."

Harper thought back, tried to squeeze more details out of the memory, but she could only come up with the low points. "I did. I do."

"Harper, please tell me you have some kind of physical evidence. Phone records. Recordings. A note in Weston's handwriting admitting culpability. Because if you don't…"

"He *told* me. His sixteen-year-old daughter. While he wept on my shoulder." Harper breathed in deep. "He tried so hard… To be a good dad. To be a success. But that investment… It broke him. When he told me, I went to hold his hand… He had a razor blade clutched in his palm. I had to pry it away from him. Don't tell Lola that part. She can't know. Ever."

She quickly glanced at Cormac to find his dark eyes on her.

Then with a growl he reached out and dragged her into his arms.

She sank into his hard embrace, the simple act of his arms around her taking the edge off the chill she didn't realise had its grip on her. He rubbed a hand up and down her back until the shakes came under control.

"He was such a sweetheart of a man, Cormac. He tried so hard… I tried so hard to make it easy for him to love us, to love me, but it wasn't enough. I wasn't enough."

Cormac shushed her softly, his breath wafting past her ear, creating new goosebumps all over her body. She turned her head till she leant against his heart.

When the silence became too much, she asked, "Do you believe me?"

He held her tighter. "I believe that you believe it. But Harper, you're making big assumptions. Distorted through the lens of a devastated teenager looking for someone to blame other than the father she adored. You have to find a way to undo this."

"Undo what?"

He breathed out hard before pulling away and looking deep into her eyes. "The grenade you just threw at Lola and Gray. The night before their wedding. You have to fix it now."

She blinked. "That's up to Lola."

"To do what?"

"To decide where her loyalties lie."

Cormac let her go so fast she stumbled, before catching herself on the back of a wrought-iron chair, the metal freezing against her hot palms.

"Weston Chadwick is a good man. A great man. The best man I've ever known. And a better father than yours and mine put together. Your accusation was serious. And Lola, Gray and I weren't the only ones to hear it. Our friends were inside. And some random bartender. Did you forget that? We can only hope the others decide to let it go. If not..."

"What? Are you going to sue me for defamation?"

His eyes flickered between hers, the muscles in his jaw working. "I am his lawyer."

"Wow. So it's come to that now." Harper began to pace, pressing a hand to her temple, which had begun to pound. "You're unbelievable."

"While you're so caught up in your own way of seeing the world you don't think. You just act. Without thought for how it affects those around you. Do you have any idea the kind of permanent damage that can cause?"

When she said nothing, Cormac shook his head. "You truly don't get it, do you? And I thought my father was self-absorbed. But you, honey, you take the cake."

"Whoa. Did you just compare me to your *father*?"

Cormac's expression was dark and sharp. Not a scrap of his usual charm. "I found your bravado enchanting. The way you see the world as something to conquer, in a way I wished I could. But you've gone over the edge here, you've gone too far. I don't know what the hell I was thinking, getting mixed up in all this."

Feeling utterly trapped, by her own words, by her feelings for Cormac, Harper lashed out. "In what, exactly?"

"This," he said, taking a step forward.

Harper gasped in a breath, her entire body bracing for his touch. Craving it.

But it never came. His mouth twitched as he held his ground.

While the empty places inside Harper filled with a rage she couldn't contain. "We aren't *doing* anything, Cormac. We made out a couple of times and rolled around on your couch. That's it."

"You're kidding me," he said, his face blank, shadowed in the semi-darkness. "That's how you see our past few days together?"

"Of course. What did you imagine would happen after tomorrow? In the time it takes for you to wax your surfboard I build and destroy companies. My life is structured. Settled. Take that house of yours. Do you not understand the pressure you put on any woman who walks through that door? It's like vodka for the ovaries. But I'm not the kind of woman who'd be content to settle down and play house. To pop out a couple of perfect, polite, high-achieving kids and imagine that will make me happy. While you…"

She took a breath.

"You might have everyone else fooled, but I saw right through the Mr Laid Back Happy Easy Charm act you have going on. You are so restless here it's a miracle you can stand still. I can feel it every time you look at me. You *yearn*, Cormac. For more, for different, for something. Only you don't know what. I know how that ends. I could never fall for a man like that."

Cormac stood so still after her tirade, she wondered if he'd heard her at all. Then his voice came to her ragged and worn as he said, "You done?"

Harper nodded.

"Then I'm glad I realised that's how you felt. Before…" He brought a hand to his mouth and turned away.

Harper swallowed, but couldn't stop herself from asking, "Before what?"

"No. You're not getting that from me too." Cormac's head dropped, his body a study in disillusionment. "I hope I'll see you tomorrow at the wedding, and only because I hope there'll be a wedding at all."

He walked towards the open doorway leading back through the games room.

What had just happened? How had that fight even begun? How had it spiraled out of control so fast? That was really it?

"Cormac," Harper called. "Cormac, come on."

But he disappeared without looking back.

"I did what I thought was best," she called, clueless as to whether anyone heard her. "I did the best I could!"

Her words wafted away on the night breeze. The taste left in her mouth bitter and acrid, leaving her feeling sick to the stomach.

The options as she'd seen them had been black and white—not tell Lola and fear for her for the rest of time, or tell her and hope she'd raised her to make smart choices.

She'd done what she thought was right.

And once again it wasn't enough.

CHAPTER TWELVE

IT WAS RIGHT on midnight by the time Cormac threw his keys onto the hall table, the clattering sound echoing in the lofty space.

He deliberately did not look into the media room, or at the cushion he'd found Harper clutching only the night before, as he marched down the hall. He didn't even bother turning on the kitchen light before he went to the fridge for a beer.

The snap of the bottle top echoed in the emptiness of the big house. "Vodka for ovaries", as Harper had called it. Cormac slowly put the drink on the bench, untouched, and gripped the cool countertop.

How the hell did she do it? Cutting straight to the heart of him. And why Harper? Why not some sweet, lovely, modest girl who kept all the contradictions she saw within him to herself?

Why? Because what would have been the point?

She was right. Cormac hadn't kept the house hoping one day his mother might come home. He'd kept it for himself.

If you build it she will come.

"She" being some imaginary woman content to settle down and play house. To pop out a couple of perfect, polite, high-achieving kids who would fit in nicely in the fantasy future he'd imagined might negate his own rotten childhood.

A fantasy was all it had been, for such a life would bore him to tears.

No wonder he'd been treading water. He'd been waiting for more. For different. For a tectonic shift. For someone who would see through him—to the good and the bad—and want him anyway.

And, like all men who ought to have been more careful in what they wished for, he'd found her.

Only he hadn't realised it until he'd seen Harper lashing out at his oldest friend, at the family who'd taken him in, and he'd chosen her side. Without thought. Without a pause. He'd stepped into her corner.

Protecting Harper had been a case of pure instinct. Protecting her from Gray and Lola. And from herself.

For she'd made a great hash of things.

He'd seen no choice but to impugn her ridiculous assertions. Even if it had meant her pushing him away. For she was too stubborn for her own good. Stubborn and fierce and so very fragile.

It had seemed better to make himself the target—for her anger, for Gray's, and for Lola's—or she'd never forgive herself.

Only now he hoped he hadn't gone too far.

Cormac picked up the beer and drank. Grimacing as the bubbles burned his throat.

He'd gone for the jugular in accusing her of acting before thinking. Of strong-arming, like his father.

When the truth was, seeing her cornered he'd been the one struggling against a ferocious rise of emotions he couldn't control.

Anger, frustration, fear; feelings he'd spent his life striving to avoid. By living simply. Wanting little. To the extreme of living in a sleepy town at the bottom of the world surrounded by people who only saw the good in him.

For in the back of his mind he'd always wondered, and worried, at what point his father had turned from a functioning man and into a monster. Was it genetic? Pre-determined? Or a slow and steady series of choices?

Despite the fact he felt as if he'd been flattened by a steamroller, the silver lining to tonight's fracas wasn't negligible. With emotions high, loyalties stretched, things could have spun so far out of control. Yet he'd kept his head. As he always did. As he always would. For those were *normal* emotions. *Human* emotions. It was the way you dealt with them that made you the man you were.

The abundant love Harper felt for her sister made her the woman she was. But tonight it had threatened to swamp her. To pull her under.

She needed to shake off her past as much as he needed to rid himself of his.

It was the only way they could move forward. Whatever that meant.

Somewhere in the house a wall creaked. A gecko made a clicking sound. His fridge began to whir. A soundtrack to loneliness.

First thing Monday he was putting the house on the market.

But what about now? Now what the hell was he supposed to do?

Go to bed and sleep it off? Not going to happen.

Not while Harper still filled his head. That burr in her voice when she'd asked if he believed her. Her body sinking into his. Her cheek against his heart.

He wondered if Harper had ever asked such a question before. Of anyone else. If she'd ever been that vulnerable with another person. He would have bet everything he had that he was the first.

Because he was more to her than a roll on the couch. And she meant more to him than anything. *Anything.*

As wrong as Harper had been, everything she'd done she'd done out of love. Knowing it could backfire. Knowing she'd be the bad guy. Knowing Lola might choose Gray, and never talk to her again. She'd been willing to sacrifice the most important thing in her life, because she believed it gave Lola a better chance at a happy future.

Which said it all really.

He ran a hand through his hair and paced down

the hall. Stopping when he had no clue where he was going. Only knowing that he had to do something.

What if there was a kernel of truth to her assumptions? What if Weston *had* been somehow involved in her father's bad deal?

If being a good person was about making hard choices then that was what Cormac would have to do.

He checked the time. A little after midnight. Too late by any stretch of the imagination, especially considering the man's only son was getting married the next day.

Yet he picked up the phone and made a call, knowing that it would change everything, no matter which way the chips fell.

Harper lay on her bed, a pillow over her head, her thumbs pressing gently into her temples.

Like gravel shifting through wet cement, she had to keep the gritty flashes of memory rolling about inside her head lest they solidify into a sharp, chunky, heavy mass she'd never be able to shift.

What had she been thinking, having that conversation the night before Lola's wedding? How could she have imagined it would go anything but badly?

Why? Because she was so used to having to make hard decisions on her own. That life had been forced upon her, when the father she'd loved had let her down.

He hadn't hit her, as Cormac's father had hit him. But he'd damaged her all the same.

A gentle knock sounded on Harper's door.

She peeked out from under the pillow to check the time on her phone and saw it was a few minutes after one in the morning. And that Lola had sent her a text a few minutes before, asking if she was awake.

She pulled herself to sitting and said, "Come in."

Her door opened slowly and Lola's face poked through the door.

"You should be asleep," Harper said, moving over to make room.

Lola crawled up Harper's bed to sit cross-legged beside her. "Like you can talk."

True. For Harper was fully dressed. Her bed still made.

"What's up?" Harper asked, finding herself unable to ask if Lola had heard her. If she'd decided to call the whole thing off. If so she'd be the bad guy and stand up in front of the crowd and tell everyone so that Lola didn't have to.

Only after the way Lola had clung to Gray, who had protected her as if she was the most precious thing in the world, the thought of the wedding not going ahead felt hollow.

"Stuff," Lola said after a while. "Thoughts.

Imaginings. Memories. Mostly of Dad. Even while I want to smack him right now for all he put us through, I still kind of wish he could be here tomorrow. Mum, too."

Harper breathed out slowly. It was the best she could do considering the lump of lead that had suddenly pressed down on her chest. She patted the pillow beside her and they lay down side by side, curled in towards one another.

"Do you remember how we used to sleep this way?" Harper asked.

"On that God-awful mattress on the floor in the rooms above the convenience store."

"The mattress was perfectly serviceable."

Lola rolled her eyes. "Always so sensitive. It was a terrible mattress. The springs dug into your back if you slept near the edge. And the apartment—do you remember the smell?"

"Mothballs."

"That's right! But it did the job of keeping us together. And I never truly thanked you for making it happen. So, thank you, Harper, for always looking out for me."

Harper felt something shift inside her at Lola's words. Shift and settle. "You're welcome."

"Now, can we agree that those days are long behind us, that you did an amazing job of raising me, even before Dad finally left, and that it's time for you to let me go?"

Harper laughed, even as a tear rolled down her

cheek, wetting the pillow. "I think I can do that. If not, I'll do my best to pretend."

"Atta girl."

She had to ask. "You're still marrying Gray, then?"

The look Lola gave her was so grown-up. "Of course I am. Whatever his father did or did not do, it does not reflect on Gray. He's his own man. My man."

Harper's mind went straight to Cormac before she could stop it.

Never, not once, had she believed that Cormac's father's actions reflected on him. Or only so far as to show how extraordinary he was, having come out the other end of such a terrible formative experience so strong, resolved, balanced, kind and loving.

It was only fair that he gave Gray the same benefit of the doubt.

"I like Gray," Harper said, and meant it.

Lola's face lit up. "Me, too." Then she said, "May I say, I've noticed signs of you having become a proper grown-up now too."

"Have you, now?"

"Apart from tonight's massive spontaneous combustion, of course. I mean, you managed to stay out of the commotion downstairs without stepping in with your negotiator hat, which was huge for you—"

"Hang on," she said. "What commotion?"

"You really didn't hear it? Dee-Dee and Weston. And Cormac."

"Cormac's back?" She'd heard his car drive away over an hour ago, kicking out gravel he'd left so fast.

Lola shook her head, and Harper's disappointment was like a living thing.

"Cormac rang Weston about an hour ago. It got loud. Heated. His voice carried all the way from the library. Knowing Gray would have fallen asleep the moment his head his pillow, I went to check on Dee-Dee then scurried downstairs to make sure Weston was okay. Only to find him talking on the phone… about Dad."

"Our dad?"

Lola nodded. "From what Dee-Dee and I could gather, he was telling Cormac everything he remembered about Dad's bad deal. Then he'd pause to listen. Then Weston would rub his forehead and try to remember more. It got pretty intense."

Harper rolled to look at the ceiling, as her heart thumped so hard it felt as if it was trying to push out of her chest. "Did he admit to anything?"

"Only that he knew of it after the fact. That he'd called Dad in, offering to help bail him out, anonymously, at least with the smaller local investors. That Dad had accepted. And that was the last time he'd seen him."

Harper breathed out long and slow.

"Harper, I believe him."

"I think I believe him too."

Yet somehow, in the quiet of the night, it didn't even matter anymore.

What mattered was Cormac. She tried to imagine what had been going through his head when he'd made that phone call. With nothing to go on but her hunch.

She knew Cormac would stand up for anyone and everyone if he thought he could help. He was just that kind of man.

But this was bigger than that. He'd stood up to his hero tonight. A man he claimed saved his life. For her.

"I've been thinking about it and I reckon I know why Dad said all that stuff about Weston," Lola said. "Dad would have been happier with a simpler life. Life in a place where keeping up with the Chadwicks wasn't a consideration. I think he'd have liked living in that one room above the convenience store with us."

That thought settled over both of them like a blanket, gathering memories as if they were dust bunnies.

On a yawn Lola said, "Not a dull moment when you're around, Harps, I'll give you that. We're going to miss you when you go back to your fancy life."

"We?"

"Me, Gray. Cormac. I think he might have a little crush on you too."

"I'll miss you all too." The thought that Cormac had already said his goodbye squeezed like a fist around her heart. "More than words can say."

But Lola had already fallen asleep, her dark lashes soft against her cheeks, her breaths even. Her little sister was going to be just fine.

As for Harper? Living out of her big, empty apartment in Dubai and spending her days bending powerful business people to her will seemed like another life. A life she'd relished. But the real satisfaction had come from it giving her the ability to give Lola everything she'd ever wanted.

Only now she realised Lola would still be happy living in a tiny flat above a convenience store. So long as she had Gray there with her.

That was what Cormac had tried to tell her. The meaning of life he'd stumbled upon at a far younger age than she had.

Find what makes you happy and do more of that.

Maybe it was time she found out what really made *her* happy.

And, as though a veil had been lifted, Harper saw the grey between the black and white. And with it a million new colours too.

Cormac, she thought, his face swimming before her as her eyes slid closed and sleep began to take her under.

So smart, so kind, so hot she couldn't even think his name without coming over all woozy and feeling like the floor was tipping out from under her.

She had to tell Cormac…something. About being best man to her maid of honour. Best man she'd ever known.

CHAPTER THIRTEEN

BY THREE THE next afternoon most of the guests were seated in gilded chairs on the Chadwicks' lawn overlooking the bluff. Others milled about, partaking in chilled flutes of local bubbly or prawn gyoza and salmon blinis.

The grass was green, the sky an uninterrupted cerulean-blue dome, the waves crashing dramatically against the jagged rocks below. Only the slightest breeze took the edge off the crisp warmth of the day.

"How you doing?" Gray asked.

Cormac came to from a million miles away, blinking against the glint of sunlight reflecting off the second-storey window at the rear of the Chadwick mansion. Harper's window.

"Me?" he said, clearing his throat of the gruff note. "Isn't that meant to be my question to you?"

Gray's smile spread slow and easy across his face. "I'm great. Looking forward to the next bit."

For Gray that might have meant seeing Lola, eating, or whisking his new bride off to Nepal—to check in with a few of the Chadwick factories and attend a surprise yoga retreat for their honeymoon. For the man was easily pleased. Cormac figured that came with being very wealthy and very loved.

Cormac had never felt that level of ease. It was why he'd had the same group of friends since high school. It took a lot for him to trust.

He looked out over the guests and caught Dee-Dee and Weston—standing shoulder to shoulder, as they always did, as if they couldn't bear to be outside of touching distance from one another—watching him.

He felt a sliver of remorse for the phone call made late the night before. Not for making the call itself—he stood by that decision. He wished he'd waited. Then maybe he'd not have come at the man with such heat, such feeling, such emotion.

Over Harper.

She provoked him like no one else. Finding soft spots, bruises he'd thought long since healed. Pressing till he was forced to say *enough*. Or to own up.

Harper.

Who'd seen that his ease, his contentment, was skin deep. When those who'd known him longest, those he'd thought had known him best, had taken his smiles at face value.

Harper.

Who had walked into his life and shaken it to pieces. Until he could no longer see it the same way he had a week before.

Dee-Dee lifted a hand, waving at him.

Cormac did the same. Then he dropped his hand over his heart, sending her his love. For she was family—if not of his blood, then in spirit.

Even from a distance he saw her smile, and her sniff, before she took a tissue from her purse and dabbed it over her eyes.

Cormac let go a long, slow breath. His life would never look the same from this day on because it wasn't.

The house he'd called a home now felt like nothing more than a roof over his head.

After the wedding the Chadwicks would announce their retirement. He'd been running their operations for years and knew they planned to make it official. He'd thought that was what he wanted. But now he wasn't so sure.

Gray and Lola would be married, meaning their lives would shoot off on a different trajectory. A life of couples' dinners and snuggling on the couch and pretty soon children. Nappies and sleepless nights. Birthday parties and scraped knees and new friends who inhabited that world.

And while a week ago such thoughts all strung together would have sent him hurtling into the surf in order to distract himself, standing beside Gray, the sun on his face, his future uncertain, Cormac felt loose. Relieved. Free.

Once more his eyes cut to the second-storey window.

To Harper.

The harpist who'd been playing rock songs at the edge of the dais stopped mid-song before launching into the opening strains of Pachelbel's Canon.

Cormac dragged his eyes back to Gray, who was busy chatting with Adele—high-school girlfriend, and current wedding celebrant. "Gray, mate, you're on."

Gray looked to Cormac blankly a moment before his eyes filled with joy. "It's happening?" he asked.

"It's happening."

Gray grabbed Cormac and yanked him into a bear hug. Cormac gave as good as he got.

"Love you, brother," Cormac managed through the tightness in his throat.

"Right back at you, brother."

Pulling apart, they turned as one to face the aisle between the gleaming gilt chairs. A path of soft pink rose petals split the guests in their floral dresses and summer suits.

The view was so bright, so cheerful, it was as if the world had been washed clean. Or that was how it looked to Cormac: fresh, new, full of possibility.

Then the doors at the rear of the house swept open and Cormac's next breath in didn't make it far. His heart beat so fast he could hear it in his ears. And Harper stepped out onto the terrace.

While the guests wore a cacophony of colour,

Harper had been poured into a subtly sexy, shimmering, pale grey number that clung to every part of her it could. Never thought he'd see the day he'd be jealous of a dress, but there it was.

Gray swore softly beside him. "If that isn't the most beautiful woman on the planet, I don't know who is."

"Hmm," Cormac murmured, in full agreement.

She looked like a dream. His dream. Dazzling on the outside, tough as nails, with a soft centre.

Then he blinked and saw the bride heading down the petal path a few steps behind her big sister.

Cormac huffed out a laugh. For Lola—a down-to-earth girl who swore, drank beer and lived in yoga pants and baseball caps—looked like a princess in the most wedding-dressy dress imaginable. And she grinned from ear to ear, showing more teeth than a person had the right to have.

As they neared the business end of the aisle, Harper slowed by Dee-Dee and Weston. She leaned over and said something, then held out her hand to Weston, who after the barest hesitation shook it heartily. While Dee-Dee leapt to her feet and hugged her for all she was worth.

If Cormac hadn't already been aware of how impressive the woman was, watching her swallow her pride and make peace with the Chadwicks pushed him right over the edge.

Gray, clueless as to the whys of the happenings, grumbled, "Can't they walk faster?"

Then, with a growl, Gray suddenly took off down the steps. Cormac reached out to grab him before deciding to let him go. The guests laughed as Gray grabbed a shocked Harper, placing a big kiss on her cheek, before running to Lola and lifting her into his arms, and rushing her back up the aisle and plonking her on the dais.

"There," he said. "Better. Let's get this thing done."

Adele's face twisted a moment before she said, "Ah, one thing's missing."

Harper had stopped in the middle of the aisle, catatonic gaze stuck on Lola, throat working, as if she didn't quite know what to do.

Cormac told Novak to stay—for the rings were hanging from a small box attached to the dog's collar—then jogged down the steps and went to Harper.

He'd planned to take her hand, and place it in the crook of his arm and lead her the rest of the way. To make it appear as if it was a part of the ceremony.

But when he caught sight of the smudge of a tear beneath her right eye, he was undone. All pretence went flying out the door.

He was done. Gone. Head over heels. He was hers—if she wanted him or not.

After the way they'd left things the night before

he couldn't be sure of the reception he'd get, so he simply followed his gut. Slipping a hand around her waist. His hand jolting when it met skin.

"What the hell?" he murmured, twisting to look at her back, to find by some kind of miraculous design it was bare from a ribbon at her neck to her lower back.

Needing every ounce of social grace he could muster, he let his hand splay over her back as he pulled her gently, fully, against him.

When her deep hazel eyes focussed on him, and she let out a sigh, some final piece shifted into place inside the new landscape of his mind.

"You ready for this?" he asked.

She shook her head.

"Yeah," he murmured. "Until about five minutes back I realised I wasn't really ready for it either. Since we're making up the rules as we go along, let's decide to get through it together."

He slid his hand an inch further around her waist, gave her a tug towards the dais. One high heel shot forward, followed by the other, and together they walked up the aisle.

Forgoing tradition, Cormac walked Harper to Lola's side and stayed there, knowing Gray didn't need his support today. Gray wouldn't have cared if a spaceship took every last person there so long as he had his girl.

And in that moment Cormac felt the same.

* * *

Once the ceremony was over the party began.

A big white tent had been filled with long farm-house tables draped in gauze and covered with every kind of food under the sun. While the band started up under an adjacent marquee.

Harper made to follow the happy couple, until Cormac took her by the elbow and dragged her off the back of the dais.

"What about the photos?"

"No set shots," Cormac said. "Photographers—plural—are moving through the crowd taking happy snaps all night long."

He really did know more about the wedding plans than she did.

"So where are we going?"

"Somewhere with less people," Cormac muttered, smiling at guest after guest who tried to flag him down.

"Can we slow down just a mite?"

He glanced back at her, his eyes hot. Dark. Too dark to read.

"This dress won't take another big step."

Cormac's gaze slid down her body, leaving spot fires in its wake. Then he slowed. "I do like that dress."

"I like your suit," she said. Though what she really meant was that she liked the man wearing it.

"Cormac—"

"Photo?"

A man with a big camera suddenly appeared in front of Harper. She squealed, and leapt into Cormac's arms.

A second later her pulled her closer and said, "No thanks." He patted his chest. "Already got one."

"One more can't hurt," said the photographer with a smile.

"Not now, mate," Cormac growled and the man slunk away. Leaving a clear run to a secluded spot beneath an oak tree at the edge of the lawn.

Once there he lined Harper up with the trunk, his hands searing through the slippery fabric of her dress before he stepped away, running his hands down the sides of his suit pants.

While she felt as if her belly was full of butterflies, her head with dust motes, Cormac looked even more discombobulated. She had to smile. "Thank you."

"Hmm?" he asked, his hand at his mouth, finger tapping manically against his bottom lip.

"For helping me through that. Seeing Lola up there, about to get married, I froze. But watching her grinning at Gray, hearing the vows they made…" Harper let out a great big sigh. "It was like watching the final piece of a puzzle fall into place."

"I know what you mean," Cormac said, focussed on her as if he couldn't bear to look away.

She remembered the revelation she'd had just before falling asleep in the early hours of that same morning. When deciding it was time to figure out what really made her happy.

Cormac's phone call to Weston had rushed through her like a waterfall of hope. The way he'd walked with her down the aisle, held her to him like something precious, looked at her as if she was the only person in the world, had given her hope wings.

Looking at Cormac looking at her now, she had no need to wonder any more.

Her voice was a little rough as she said, "Why did you pat your jacket when the photographer asked to take our picture?"

He looked at her then, face blank. Not a tell in sight. But she knew him too well. "Come on, Cormac, fess up."

His mouth curved at one corner, and her heart flipped over on itself. "You really can see right through me, can't you? I'm going to have to remember that in future."

In future. Meaning he saw a future between them.

She shook her head, even while every other part of her was saying yes, yes, yes! "Stop trying to distract me." She reached for his jacket, flapping open the lapel and patting the inner lining. "What are you hiding in here?"

Her fingers slipped into the pocket and came out with—

"Oh."

For inside Cormac's jacket was the thin strip of black and white pictures of the two of them together, taken by the photo booth at the bucks' and hens' night.

"Where did you get these?"

"I grabbed them the moment they were taken."

"And you kept them?"

His face softened, his expression indulgent. *Of course I kept them, Harper.*

"Why have you got them on you today?"

"I've had them on me ever since that night." He lifted his hand, placing it over the now empty pocket. Over his heart.

She looked down at the pictures. In the first image she looked so stressed. While he looked straight out gorgeous, with his knee-melting smile and warm eyes.

In the second she appeared exasperated. While he looked as if he was having too much fun.

In the third... That was right. He had kissed her on the cheek. Her mouth had sprung open, and her eyes were wide with surprise.

In the last picture she had turned to chastise him, only to give him prime opportunity to kiss her. Gently. Sweetly. Lips only just touching. Her eyes had fluttered closed, her whole body was leaning into his and her hand gripped his shirt.

And even in the grainy black and white, and all the shades of grey in between, she could see his smile.

She ran a thumb over the image. To think that woman in the picture—the woman giving herself so freely, so completely, so honestly, so vulnerably—was really her.

"About last night," she said, taking a moment to choose her words carefully. For the consequences were great. "I said some things, a great many things, that weren't exactly true. Or, maybe to be more precise, do not rightly explain how I feel."

"About?"

She looked up to find him standing before her—one hand in his trouser pocket, the other resting by his side. So handsome her heart ached.

"About you."

He breathed in deep, and waited for her to go on.

"I fear I might have made you think that you meant nothing more to me than a couple of kisses."

"And a roll on the couch, don't forget," he said, ambling closer. Sunlight dappling his suit through the leaves above. Playing shadow and light across his face. "I believe those were your exact words."

"Mmm… So they were."

"Are you suggesting you may have misrepresented your feelings?"

The man was a master at word play, probably what made him such a great lawyer, but Harper was a go-getter at heart. And if she didn't get soon she might spontaneously combust.

"Big time," she said.

His eyes flared with heat. His gaze drifting over her face before settling on her mouth.

"I've been fighting it since the moment I saw you sitting on the hood of your ridiculously romantic car. Heck, I've been fighting it since you walked the halls of Blue Moon Bay High, a smile on your face, a whistle as you walked, giving yourself to anyone and everyone in your path. I can't fight it any more. And I won't. I'm in love with you, Cormac."

His gaze, which had been roving over her dress as if trying to figure out a way to get through it one stitch at a time, lifted to her eyes.

Then he came to her in three strides, his hand reaching behind her neck as he pulled her to him and kissed her like a man drowning, and she the last drink of water on earth. When she moaned, and pressed herself all up against him, he wrapped an arm around her back and hefted her into his arms.

Aeons later the kisses slowed, softened, until they clung to one another with the barest touch of their lips.

"You love me," he said, his voice rough.

"Like nothing else. I've never felt that way before. But I know it. I know it like I know my own name."

"I believe you."

"You do?"

He nodded, his forehead sliding over hers. Then he slowly lifted his face away, his gaze snagging on hers. He slid her hair from her face, then traced the edge of her jaw. All the while looking at her as if he couldn't believe she was real.

She said, "I don't expect you to—"

He leaned down and silenced her with one more kiss. The kind that made a girl's knees forget how to work.

Then, reaching for her, cupping her cheeks, he looked from one eye to the other and said, "Harper, you must know that I'm in love with you too."

Harper swallowed lest she let out the sob that threatened to undo her completely. Then she threw her arms around his neck and held on tight.

In the distance people chatted, music played, food was devoured, and Lola and Gray's wedding party went on as if the entire world had not shifted beneath their feet. As if the boy Harper had a crush on all those years ago, the one whose smile had given her respite from the craziness of home, hadn't just told her he loved her.

As she pressed her face to his shoulder, as he held her tight, she laughed out loud.

"What's so funny?"

"I'm leaving tomorrow, Cormac. I have a plane to catch and contracts to fulfil." It all felt so insig-

nificant compared with this, but she'd made promises. She'd never been one to walk away from a
commitment and wasn't about to start now.

"While the Chadwicks are retiring and plan to
announce my taking over as CEO of Chadwick
Corp."

Harper leant back the better to see his face. To
check if he was as indifferent to the idea as he
sounded. "Cormac, that's amazing!"

"I'm not taking it on."

"Why on earth not?"

He grinned. Shook his head. "Only you would
show your regret at having to leave all this then
berate me for feeling the same way."

"Why?" she asked, slapping him on the chest.
"Talk to me."

"You know why."

Harper lifted a hand to her chest. "You're giving
it up…for me? No. You will not sacrifice something you've worked your whole life for, for me."

"Why not?"

"I'm not…" She swallowed the words that had
been about to leave her mouth. Words she'd spent
her entire life telling herself she didn't believe.

"You are more than enough, Harper. You're everything. To me. I can see your brain whirling,
and I need you to stop. To listen, to believe me
when I say that this is what I want. I'm going out
on my own. Going to use that mighty education
of mine to do good. I can start with pro bono for

some of the Chadwick charities. Then reinstate my licence to practise in the UK. Or the United Arab Emirates, perhaps. It's been a while since I've been to Dubai."

Harper swallowed, the world so bright and shiny and colourful she had to squint. "But you love your job."

"I love doing good work that satisfies me. The Chadwicks will be fine. I'll even help them scour the world for someone amazing to fill the position. Or who knows, it might even light a fire under Gray, give him the chance to take on his birth right."

"Or not," Harper said.

Cormac grinned, and ran a finger over her forehead, trying to smooth out the frown. "So what do you say?"

"I say… Okay!" she said, her voice light as air.

"Okay?"

"Yes. Okay. To everything. Anything. We've been making up the rules as we went along, so why stop now? I want you to come with me. As soon as you can. And I want to come back here, too. As often as possible. To see Lola more. To get to know Dee-Dee and Weston and Gray. For if they love Lola and they love you then they can't be all bad."

"Who loves me?" Cormac asked, feigning deafness in his right ear.

"I do."

"What was that? I missed it."

"I love you, Cormac Wharton," she said throwing her arms out and shouting for the whole world to hear. "Cutest boy in school. Hottest man in town. Did I mention how much I like you in that suit?"

He brushed a stray lock of hair behind her ear, his eyes following the move, his fingers delving into her hair, cupping the back of her head and staying there. Then his gaze swept back to hers. "I love you too, Harper Addison. You stubborn, fierce, mercurial, gorgeous creature. Did I mention stubborn?"

"Since we met again? Several times."

Cormac leaned down and kissed her right as she lifted onto her toes and kissed him, the photos that somehow magically tracked the course of their relationship in four frames clutched in her hand.

"Do you think it's time we headed back?" he asked, lips brushing against hers.

She shook her head, even as she said, "Yes. We'd better."

He slung an arm about her shoulders and pulled her close and together they made their way back to the wedding party. Slowly.

"So this crush of yours," he said.

"Mmm?"

"Do you think it might last this time?"

"I think it might."

"Hmm. That's what I was afraid of."

Harper tipped her head to his shoulder. "Any advice on what we can do about it?"

"I have a couple of ideas," he said, his voice muffled as he kissed the top of her head. "Actually, more than a couple. A veritable cornucopia. As far as I see it, we'll have to work our way through them until I've exhausted you. I mean, your crush."

Harper couldn't wait. "Confident, much?"

"Are you suggesting I have no reason to be?"

Harper spun out from under his arm, taking his hand in both of hers as she walked backwards near the edges of the party.

"Please," she said, pretending to chew gum as she affected her most 'high school' voice. "You're not all that, Cormac Wharton."

He lifted an eyebrow in patent disagreement.

Fine, she thought. He was all that and more.

How much more she could not wait to find out.

EPILOGUE

Cormac turned off the upstairs shower, muscles eased from the hard, hot spray, feeling a little more alive despite the lack of sleep the night before.

He'd have to do something about that. About the fact he couldn't keep his hands off Harper. He was a fit guy, running now since surf wasn't as close to home anymore, but even he needed some sleep in order to be a functioning member of society.

At some point he'd do something about it. Not now. Now things were pretty much perfect. Not that he'd say that to his girl. She was so determined to believe perfection was an impossibility. It could be his secret to bear.

He grabbed his toothbrush and brushed, thinking about the text he'd send Harper when she got to the airport.

Though she was heading into the restaurant on the way. Her company's first ever investment—a small elegant Italian seafood joint down the road from their new Chelsea digs.

She was a silent partner with an ex-client and his son. Or had they been opponents in a contract dispute just before she'd come home to Blue

Moon Bay? He'd never quite been able to get the gist. Apparently they'd sold up a string of restaurants but Harper had convinced them that with her help they could create something wonderful, something new.

Though he wasn't sure she'd grasped the *silent* part, as she visited every time she was in back in London, pored over the financials, the contracts with suppliers, making damn sure it remained efficient and in the black.

And the place was doing great. The father and son who ran it seemed really happy, so he let her be.

Especially since she seemed really happy too.

Grinning as he wiped condensation from the mirror, he stopped his hand mid-swipe when he heard Harper's voice. Raised, in frustration.

Cormac grabbed his towel, wrapped it quickly around his waist and took off out the bathroom door, down the stairs and out the front door.

It was a summer's day in London, which was nothing like a summer's day back home, and Cormac's toes curled at the chill that met his bare feet.

Cormac could hear Harper's voice, strident and sure, coming from the miniscule front garden but he couldn't see her at all.

It had only been a matter of time before some neighbour made the mistake of trying to tell her where to park the Sunbeam, or how high to let the roses grow, clueless as to the fact they'd be dealing with the Negotiator.

Thankfully he was known for his charm, and was ready to leap in and clean up the mess.

"Harper?"

After a beat, she said, "Down here."

He bent over the railing to find her on her hands and knees on the grass, one sexy high heel poking out from behind her skirt-clad backside. Cormac fixed his towel and leant on a newel, prepared to put up with the cold when it came with such a view.

"Come on, sweet puppy," Harper cajoled. "Give it to me."

Her Maltese terrier pup, Marnie, stood about a metre away, Harper's other shoe hanging from her mouth. They'd engaged in a battle of wills ever since Harper had brought her home. But they were besotted with one another at the same time.

Novak watched on from the sidelines, though after seeing Cormac she ambled up the stairs and leant against his leg.

Cormac made a kiss-kiss noise. Marnie's ears pricked before she came bolting up to him, dropped the shoe and jumped around on her back feet.

Cormac lifted her up, gave her a kiss, then plopped her back inside the house, shutting the door behind her.

Harper blew a stream of air from the side of her

mouth then pulled herself to her feet. Or, more precisely, her foot. "Of course, the dog has a crush on you too."

Cormac grinned and held up a shoe with a heel that could take out a vampire. "Looking for this?"

Harper limped up the stairs, fixing her suit as she went. And, hell, if he didn't want to drag her inside and unfix it. But he knew she wouldn't want to miss visiting the restaurant on the way to the airport, so he leaned down to help her on with her shoe, before sliding a hand up her leg, up her hip, around her back and pulling her in for a kiss.

A car horn beeped as a black cab pulled up just beyond their gate.

Harper's gaze was gorgeously fuzzy as she pulled away slowly from his kiss. "Two more days in New York to get this contract to bed. Then I'll be home tomorrow night. I have nothing lined up after this so I'm all yours for as long as you want me."

"I'll be waiting with bated breath till you come home."

"Right here?" she asked, her hand going to his towel and giving it a quick tug.

"I won't move an inch."

She pressed up against him a little more, and he moved more than an inch.

Knowing she was close to fulfilling the contracts she'd had in place after Lola and Gray's wedding, he'd cleared his schedule as well. "Since we have a rare break in the calendar, how about we go home."

She blinked. "Home-home?"

They hadn't been back to Blue Moon Bay in six months, and he knew she was itching to see Lola even more than he was ready to see his friends and family.

Cormac nodded. "Winter will have hit Blue Moon Bay by now. The fires will be lit. We can rug up against the brisk wind coming in off the bay."

Harper breathed out hard. "Yes, please. But what about—?"

"Adele and Wilma will look after the dogs." Adele had hooked up with one of Lola's yoga-teacher friends at the wedding, an English girl, and had made the trek north not long after Harper and Cormac had done the same. "It'll be a Hampstead holiday for them too."

"Gotta love a man who thinks of everything."

"Love you too." And saying it to this woman never got old. "We'll head off at the end of the week, giving you just enough time to pack."

The cab driver beeped again. Harper turned and shot the driver a look. He lifted his hands in surrender, grabbed a magazine and hunkered down in his seat.

"Go," Cormac said, reaching down to hand her her small suitcase from the landing.

She gave him a quick kiss. Then reached around

his neck to give him a kiss hotter than any summer's day he'd ever known.

While he fixed his towel, Harper jogged down the stairs in her killer heels, slid into the cab and was gone.

Cormac watched the car till it turned the corner. Breathed in a lungful of London air, before heading inside, Novak at his heels.

He didn't tell her the flights had been booked weeks before.

Or that he'd tracked down the photo booth from Lola and Gray's party, and paid an exorbitant amount of money to have it waiting for him in the Chadwicks' pool house.

That it was plugged in, stocked with film, ready and waiting for Cormac to lead Harper inside.

For there was where he planned to offer her the diamond ring he'd had sitting in his sock drawer for months. Where he would ask her to be his wife.

Grinning from the inside out, Cormac hit the kitchen to grab an apple. And glanced at the strip of black and white photo-booth photos stuck to their fridge. Photos of Harper looking stressed, then frustrated, surprised, then melting into his kiss, while in every picture he looked like a man who was happy to wait for his girl to catch up.

He moved them over a little to make room for the new strip he'd bring back once their trip home was done. Pictures he had no doubt would show two people crazy in love.

It's a big fridge, Cormac thought, and he couldn't wait to fill it with photos of his family. And friends.

And Harper. His woman. His love. His everything.

Upstairs Cormac went; a man with a plan, a smile on his face, and a whistle as he walked.

* * * * *

If you enjoyed this story,
check out these other great reads
from Ally Blake

Hired by the Mysterious Millionaire
Amber and the Rogue Prince
Rescuing the Royal Runaway Bride
Millionaire Dad's SOS

All available now!